"It looks like someone is trying to sabotage my efforts to make a nice home for these girls. What I can't figure out is why."

Detective Reece Corrigan scowled. "That's what I'm here for, and I have to tell you—"

Denni raised her hand to stop him. "What possible motive could any of my girls have to sabotage their own home? Where would they go?"

Leaving him to mull that over, she marched to the top of the stairs. He followed her into the kitchen.

"That's the one thing I can't put my finger on. It doesn't make a lot of sense, but maybe the person we're dealing with here doesn't think along rational lines."

"All my girls are rational," Denni snapped.

His amusement was more than apparent in the upward curve of his lips. "Then I guess they must take after you," he drawled.

* * *

The Mahoney Sisters: Fighting for justice and love.

Books by Tracey V. Bateman

Love Inspired Suspense

Reasonable Doubt #4
Suspicion of Guilt #6

*The Mahoney Sisters

TRACEY V. BATEMAN

lives in Missouri with her husband and their four children. She writes full-time and is active in various roles in her home church. She has won several awards for her writing, and credits God's grace and a limited number of entries for each win. To relax, she enjoys long talks with her husband, reading and music and hanging out with her kids, who can finally enjoy movies she likes. Tracey loves to encourage everyone to dream big. She believes she is living proof that, with God, nothing is impossible.

Tracey V. Bateman

Suspicion of Guilt

Steeple
Hill®

Published by Steeple Hill Books™

STEEPLE HILL BOOKS

Steeple
Hill®

ISBN 0-373-44222-X

SUSPICION OF GUILT

Copyright © 2005 by Tracey V. Bateman

Printed in U.S.A.

You watched me as I was being formed
in utter seclusion, as I was woven together in the
dark of the womb. You saw me before I was born.
Every day of my life was recorded in your
book. Every moment was laid out before
a single day had passed.
—*Psalms* 139:15–16

This book is dedicated to my precious friend Nancy Scott, who believes in the mandate for older (though she is *not* old) women to teach the younger women. God used you to teach me that I was somebody in His eyes. Thank you for sharing the theme scripture of this book with me when I was a teenager.

Special thanks to my faithful critique partners as always—especially Chris Lynxwiler and Pamela Griffin; both of you stayed by your computers to get chapters from me to critique on the spur of the moment so that I wouldn't miss my deadline. Only God could have given me such loyal friends.

Also, thanks to my mother, Frances Devine, and to my mother-in-law, Vivian Bateman. Thank you both for believing in my dreams enough to sacrifice your time so that I can put mine to the best use during the days of deadline mania. May God bless you both abundantly above all you could ever ask or think.

Thank you, Jesus. It's all about You.

Prologue

The night swirled around her. Black, stabbing darkness conjured terrible shadows from childhood nightmares. Leaves hovered like a vampire's cape, suffocating. Fear gripped her. Branches tossed in the breeze—razor-sharp fingers ready to slice her to shreds.

Hurry, hurry, hurry.

A low half growl, half whine came from the Doberman behind the fence next door. She jerked her head at the sound, heart pounding in her ears like the thrum of a thousand drums.

Shh. "It's okay," she whispered. *Don't give me away. I'm so close to accomplishing my goal.* The dog obeyed and sat—watching but silent.

Relief flooded her as she turned back to her task. Denni Mahoney, with all of her sweetness and light...

Shards of rage pierced her heart at the thought of Denni getting what she wanted. She didn't deserve it. A mastermind of deception. Denni had fooled them all.

Everyone but me. The thought made her smile with grim determination.

With a shaky hand, she reached for the outside faucet. Hesitated. One twist and the broken pipe would send water rushing inside the house instead of flowing to the ground. The basement would flood.

She grasped the faucet tightly and gave it a quick turn. Water spewed.

The Doberman barked.

Her heart rate escalated. She pushed to her feet, gulping down the fear and crept across the yard. Exultation shoved away the terror of night as she found safety.

Chapter One

Shock, disbelief, horror…all vied for first place in Denni Mahoney's chest as she stared at the foot of water standing in her basement. Water. Just…standing there where water was never meant to be. She shook her head, pressing her palm to her forehead.

What next?

"We'll get to the bottom of this." Behind her, Detective Reece Corrigan's tone was hard-edged, resolute, but the warmth of his hand on her shoulder evoked a strange sense of comfort.

"You have to admit it definitely could be one of them. Why do you insist that all five of the girls are innocent?"

The warm, comforting fuzzies turned to cold stone. She didn't have to admit any such thing, and she was sick of his suspicions being centered on the girls. Anger shoved down the tears clogging her throat, and she shook off his hand.

Standing on the fourth step from the bottom of the basement stairs, Denni watched a hardback book float across the water covering the concrete floor. *A Tale of*

Two Cities. A birthday gift from her mom when she'd turned fifteen. Little by little her memories of Mom were being destroyed. It had been ten years since her death, and only photos provided a clear picture of her face anymore.

Denni grimaced and turned away, but Reece's body on the step above her blocked the flight up. Even when she sent him her fiercest frown, he didn't budge.

She drew in the subtle scent of his spicy aftershave. Understated appeal. She liked that about him. The guy had to know what he did to women—a worked-out physique and a masculinity that intimidated Denni, yet left her silently wishing he'd stay close. She eyed his muscled arms and broad chest and couldn't help but wonder what it might feel like to be drawn close. To lose herself in a comforting embrace.

"Well?" he asked, the tension in his voice replaced by a subtle, low tone that seeped over her like a gentle rain.

She gaped, fighting the warmth creeping to her cheeks. "Well what?"

"I'm going to have to question them again. Who should I speak with first this time?"

"Oh, Reece," she said, hearing the fatigue in her tone. She was so tired. So very, very tired. "Leave the girls alone, will you? How can you blame them for a flood?"

Her girls. Troubled, ex-foster-care kids who were too old to stay in the system, but too young to be out on their own. As a social worker, she had grown tired of seeing so many of these girls end up on public assistance, their own children placed in foster care, so she'd cleaned out her savings account, cashed in some bonds and opened a home.

Only five young women lived with her, but if her experiment panned out, she had commitments from several local churches to help buy two more homes, each housing ten girls. Monday, she was supposed to host a luncheon for the liaisons from each of these churches. How could she explain to potential sponsors that the cops suspected the residents of sabotage?

Denni glanced back at the basement, searching for escape from the confrontation that was surely to come. It was either hike down the steps and swim through the murky water or face Reece's solid stubbornness. She sighed, knowing there was only one logical choice. She'd have to face him.

Forcing herself away from the sight of so many of her treasures soaked and more than likely ruined, she braced for the coming conflict, a tiresome, constant echo of accusation.

Deliberately, she lifted her gaze and faced sharp green eyes. Steely, knee-weakening eyes that raked over her face, commanding her to accept the possibility.

"Admit it," he demanded.

"I admit only one thing. It looks as though someone is trying to sabotage my efforts to make a nice home for these girls." A sigh pushed from her lungs. "What I can't figure out is why."

Detective Corrigan scowled. "That's what I'm here for, and I have to tell you…"

Denni raised her hand to stop the opinion from flying out of his mouth. "What possible motive could any of them have to sabotage their own home? Where would they go?"

Leaving him to mull over that bit of reason, she scraped against his bomber jacket as she maneuvered around him and marched to the top of the stairs. He followed her into the kitchen.

"That's the one thing I can't put my finger on. It doesn't make a lot of sense, but maybe the person we're dealing with here doesn't think along rational lines."

"*All* my girls are rational," Denni snapped.

His amusement was more than apparent in the upward curve of his lips. "Then I guess they must take after you," he drawled.

Fighting the urge to stomp away like a five-year-old, Denni snatched up the phone and dialed the number for the electric company.

She scowled at Reece, just as a lady on the other end answered, effectively cutting off any retort. "Hello, this is Denni Mahoney at 344 Clark Street. My basement flooded. I need someone to shut off my electricity while we pump it out."

"One moment, please."

Denni drummed her nails along the Formica cabinet top wishing Detective Corrigan would just stop staring at her like that. "What?" she snapped, shooting him a hard glance.

"I beg your pardon?" The lady on the phone sounded mildly irritated.

"Sorry, I wasn't talking to you."

Corrigan smirked. Denni turned her back.

"Ma'am, I'm told all you need to do is shut off the circuits to the basement."

Denni closed her eyes and shook her head. She pressed her fingertips to her temple. Did she look like an idiot or just sound like one over the phone? "Yeah, the problem with that advice is that my breaker box is actually *in* the basement, and I'm not real thrilled with the idea of getting zapped."

"Oh."

Yeah, *Oh.*

"All right. I'll have someone come over first thing Monday morning."

"Wait! Monday? I have *water* in my *basement!* I can't wait until Monday."

"Yes, ma'am. I understand that. But that's the earliest time we have available. The last orders have already gone out for the day. And we don't work on the weekends."

Denni bit back a nasty reply and hung up. She smacked the counter with her palm. "What am I supposed to do until Monday with water soaking my basement?"

"Stay upstairs?" Corrigan's attempt at humor spiked her irritation level.

She glared. "Not funny." Besides the question was rhetorical.

"Sorry," he muttered. "Do you want to talk about all of this?"

"No."

"Then why did you call me?"

She shrugged. Why *had* she called him? She'd walked down the steps this morning to do a load of laundry, discovered the flooded basement, and all she could think to do was call Reece. It made no sense to her.

"I'll tell you why. Because you know that a creek in your basement is no accident." He looked past her and his eyes clouded.

A feminine voice, thick with disdain, shot through the air before Denni could confirm or deny his assumption. "Oh, great. What's *he* doing here?"

Denni snapped her head around at the anger in

Leigh's tone. The girl leaned jauntily against the door frame, thumbs latched in her front jeans pockets. With her short spiked hair dyed pitch-black, and sporting a lip ring and a belly shirt, the girl looked a little wild, but Denni knew the softy inside. Reece on the other hand looked like a tiger about to spring.

"So, where have you been all day?" he asked.

"None of your business." She dismissed him with a sneer and turned to Denni. "What happened?"

"Someone left the outside faucet on."

Leigh groaned. "Oh, great! Not again. I'll go hook up the wet 'n' dry vac."

"Don't bother. We'll have to get it pumped out. It's pretty deep."

Leigh kicked at the linoleum with one socked foot. "How much is that going to cost?"

"Nothing." Corrigan's voice cut through the air. "I know a guy with a pump."

As much as Denni wanted to believe in his good intentions, the offer had the distinct odor of a rat. A big fat suspicious rat with a shiny badge and knee-weakening green eyes.

"Thanks, anyway."

"Yeah. Who needs you?" Leigh growled in his direction.

Denni couldn't blame the girl for her animosity. Since the first mishap three months ago—a laptop computer and a pretty expensive stereo system both missing—Corrigan had made no secret of the fact that he wasn't ruling out any of the girls as suspects. Leigh had seemed to take the brunt of his questions. A fire in the laundry room a month later had only deepened his suspicion. Especially after he'd found a lighter and cigarettes in her room. And no amount of don't-judge-a-book-by-its-cover speeches from Denni could deter him.

"Come on," he said. "No strings attached."

Leigh snorted. "Yeah, right."

He shrugged. "Suit yourself, but these guys work by the hour. Who knows how long it'll take to pump out that much water?"

"We'll manage, Detective," Denni said, mentally calculating how much was left in her account, and if worse came to worst, her credit-card balances.

"Fine. At least come down and fill out a report."

Denni shook her head. "I've changed my mind. It was probably just an accident."

"Sure." His lips dripped with sarcasm. "A water faucet that only your girls know is broken. Why would anyone else have turned it on?"

"I don't know."

He gave a frustrated huff. "If you'd report it, I'd be officially assigned to investigate. We could get to the bottom of this."

"Hey, Corrigan," Leigh piped in. "Where's our stereo and computer? Weren't you assigned to that one, too?"

"Can it, Leigh," Denni said. There was no sense in antagonizing him.

Too late. The guy was sufficiently ticked off. He took a step toward the sneering girl. "Why don't you tell me who you sold them to? Then I'll get them back for Denni."

"Why don't you stop trying to be a big shot and just do your job?"

Denni cringed as the gloves officially came off. These two were going for a knockout.

"Believe me, I'm doing my job, little girl. And unless I miss my guess, you'll be finding that out first-hand, real quick."

"Are you threatening me?"

"Good grief." Denni smacked the counter again, heedless of the stinging in her palm. "You two are acting like a couple of three-year-olds. Detective, is there anything else we can do for you?" Belatedly she remembered *she'd* called *him.*

She cringed as his brow went up. "No, I don't guess there's anything else I want, but I recognize an invitation to leave when I hear one. I'll show myself out." He brushed past Leigh. "I'll be seeing you soon."

"I can't wait," she smarted back.

"Good bye, Detective," Denni said. "Thank you for the offer of the pump."

"Yeah, no problem." He gave her a long stare, then shook his head and stalked out of the kitchen.

"What a weasel."

Reece's lips twisted into a wry grin at Leigh's assessment of his charm—or the lack thereof. He paused on the other side of the wall separating him from the kitchen, feeling like a jerk for eavesdropping, but thinking he might be handed a clue on a silver platter if he hung out at the door for awhile.

"We don't have time to think about him right now, Leigh," Denni's voice responded. "What am I going to do about Monday's luncheon?"

"Oh, brother. I forgot about that."

Luncheon? The woman had a serial saboteur on her hands and she was giving a party? Reece scowled.

Leigh's voice continued. "Who can we call to get the basement pumped out?"

"There's no point. The electric company won't shut off the electricity until Monday."

"Well, that's that."

Denni's sigh went straight to Reece's heart. He shook it off. Now was not the time to get soft about the house mother. For all he knew, she might be the one responsible for the mishaps. He'd have to look into her insurance policy again.

In the meantime, she was going to take his help whether she wanted it or not.

He lifted his cell phone from his belt and dialed while he walked to his truck, a gray and black Avalanche. He leaned against the door listening to the rings.

"Hey, Jack," he said when his friend answered the phone. "I have a little problem I need some help with."

"What's that?"

"How hard would it be to get a rush order to shut off someone's electricity?"

"What kind of police work calls for you to do that?"

"None. This is a personal favor. The lady has a basement full of water and can't pump it out while the electricity is on."

He hesitated a minute. "Give me the address and I'll see what I can do."

"Thanks, Jack. Oh, one more thing. Can you turn it back on tomorrow? She has a luncheon on Monday."

A knowing chuckle reached his ears. "Hey, don't tell me you finally found someone who actually wants to go out with you."

Heat burned his neck. The idea of dating Denni Mahoney had merit. As a matter of fact, he'd thought of it more than once. And if the case ever wrapped up, he might ask her out, but not now. "No. Nothing like that." He gave him the address and quickly disconnected the call.

Before he could lift the door handle and climb into the truck, a low growl caught his attention, setting his senses on high alert.

With careful movement, he turned his head. A Doberman stood not five feet away, teeth bared, and looking ready to bite a hunk out of him.

"Easy, boy."

"Buffy! Leave that man alone!"

Buffy? This had to be the worst case of misnaming an animal he'd ever encountered. Boy or girl, Buffy looked more like a Bruiser or a Spike.

Still he felt a little embarrassed to have been so antsy, when an elderly woman marched right up to the dog and smacked it on the nose as though Buffy didn't have the capacity to bite off a thumb. "Shame on you," she scolded. "What have I told you about being nasty to people?"

Buffy's pink tongue shot out and lathered the woman's wrinkled hand. She melted visibly. "Oh, you're such a sweetie pie," she crooned.

"Ma'am. I take it this is your dog?"

"Of course, she is. Aren't you, Buffy Boo?"

Reece tensed. The baby talk was getting on his nerves. Flashing his badge, he put on his best off-duty-but-still-a-cop face. "Inside the city limits, Buffy has to stay behind a fence or inside the house where she isn't a threat to anyone."

"Buffy wouldn't hurt a fly."

"The behavior I just witnessed was pretty aggressive, ma'am. I thought I might have to pepper-spray her."

The woman gasped then frowned, causing deep furrows between her eyes. "Nothing more than police brutality."

Reece scowled. All he needed was a woman on the verge of hysteria over her vicious dog.

He was about to leave her with a simple warning to get the dog secured somehow, when she pointed her shaky, gnarled finger at him. "My Buffy is the only protection I have from the neighborhood thugs and thieves." She jerked her head toward Mahoney House. "Do you know who lives there?" she asked in a hoarse whisper. "Juvenile delinquents." The smug look she gave him clearly stated that she need say no more. "They come and go at all hours of the night with their earrings and spiked hair."

Against all reason, Reece found his defenses creeping upward. "Ma'am. I'm not in the habit of harassing elderly ladies and their guard dogs. However, the law states all dogs be kept secured. You can't leave her out even if you don't approve of your neighbors. Is that clear?"

Anger shot through her faded blue eyes. "I'll put her back behind her fence, but I can't guarantee she won't get loose and go after one of them."

"Let's hope that doesn't happen."

The lady snorted and tugged on Buffy's collar. "Come on sweet 'ums. Let's get you home and give you some food."

Squinting against the sun's reflection off the back of his truck, Reece watched her leave, Buffy in tow. Now, there was a woman with a reason to get Mahoney House closed down. Why hadn't Denni ever mentioned trouble with her neighbors?

Making a mental note to do some more investigating, Reece climbed behind the wheel and cranked the engine. This case was bizarre. It irked him that so many months had gone by without a crack. Robbery and sabotage? How did the two of them go hand in hand?

He had figured one of the girls had lifted the electronics from the house and sold them for quick cash, but Denni had a point. What reason would they have for flooding the basement of their own home? The neighbor, on the other hand, might have a reason for sabotage, but the thought of that little old lady sneaking into the house and pilfering almost made him laugh. Not that it was completely impossible, but it was improbable and certainly not something he'd want to bring up to his chief.

He glanced at Mahoney House. A curtain dropped as though someone had been watching him. Denni? He smiled, but dismissed the likelihood. It was a nice little fantasy to boost his ego, anyway.

Two hours later, he was on his way back to the Mahoney House with a borrowed portable pump and a generator in the back of his truck.

The electricity should be off by now and he had Jack's word that he'd turn it back on tomorrow evening. Reece wasn't helping out just to be a nice guy. This was also his way of spending time with the girls in their own environment. Something he'd never had the chance to do before. Maybe he could earn their trust. And someone would start talking.

The added bonus was the time he would spend with Denni Mahoney. His throat constricted at the thought. From their first rocky meeting, he'd been attracted to her despite the circumstances. With round eyes the color of melted chocolate, sweet perfume, shiny hair and soft curves, she was the embodiment of beauty and feminin-

ity. Alluring enough to warm a man's blood, yet innocent enough for him to picture her in a white wedding
gown carrying a bouquet at the same time.

The memory of her eyes flashing with anger when
she defended the girls made him grin. She was spunky
to boot. He was determined to find the person responsible for trying to thwart her dream. So far, trying to be
the hard-edged cop hadn't drawn out the saboteur.
Maybe it was time to turn on the charm.

Chapter Two

Peeking from behind the burgundy drapes hanging at the living-room window, Denni felt her heart jump at the sight of Reece's truck pulling into the drive.

In a way, she wanted to ask him, "Hey, what part of 'no' don't you understand, buddy?" But mostly, she wanted to throw her arms around him and thank him for taking matters into his own hands and not accepting no for an answer.

"What's he doing back here?" Leigh's voice next to Denni arrested her attention, pulling her from the vision of flying into Reece's well-muscled arms.

"Looks like he decided to help us clean up whether we like it or not."

Leigh headed for the door—all bad attitude and body language. "Want me to get rid of him?"

"No, don't be rude. He's doing us a favor." Just why he was doing them a favor, she didn't know. But she wasn't opposed to figuring it out.

"I think it's sort of sweet." Denni turned at the soft sound of Cate Sheridan's voice. The girl waddled across the room, her eight-months-pregnant belly leading the way.

"Sweet?" Leigh sniffed. "Those hormones are definitely affecting your brain. The guy's been on our backs for months accusing us of robbing Denni. Now he's blaming us for a flood. And you think he's sweet?"

"Crazy, isn't it?" Cate grinned and elbowed Denni. "He sure is a hottie, don't you think?"

Warmth flooded Denni's cheeks. It was one thing for her to consider Reece a good-looking man in the privacy of her own mind, another for the girls to notice. She rolled her eyes and tried to recover some dignity. "I'm too old to think 'hottie' when I see a guy."

"Yeah, right." Leigh's voice held no humor.

Cate nudged Denni again and said in her best Southern drawl, "Ya might be old, honey. But ya ain't dead."

Denni couldn't hold back a laugh.

Obviously seeing nothing funny about the whole situation, Leigh swept over them both with a glare. "Just remember this particular guy is out for my blood, Denni. Don't let him charm you into suspecting one of us."

Denni turned to the girl, and her heart softened at the worry darkening Leigh's black-lined eyes. "Leigh, I know you had nothing to do with any of the things that have happened around here. And it would take a lot more than a great-looking guy with big muscles to make me believe any different."

"You say that now. But you don't know guys all that well, Denni. My mom used to run off with every charmer that came along until he'd dump her, then she'd take up with another one. And my mom isn't a stupid woman. These guys are good talkers. Believe me, they know how to get what they want from a woman. Especially one as nice as you."

Three sharp raps on the door stopped Denni from pursuing the conversation. Leigh rarely talked about her biological mother. Perhaps she was almost ready to open up. But with Reece standing in the doorway, Leigh's entire demeanor spoke of belligerence and the polar opposite of cooperation. Denni knew there would be no getting the girl to talk today.

"What do you want, Corrigan?" Leigh demanded.

"It's all right." Denni moved forward quickly in an effort to avoid an unpleasant scene. "I understand you're to thank for getting the electric company to shut off the power for us."

He gave a modest grin and nodded as he stepped inside. "I overheard Miss Sommers mention your luncheon on Monday."

"Eavesdropper," Leigh accused.

"Yes," Denni said firmly. "And thanks to his eavesdropping, we can get the basement cleaned up and perhaps pull off the luncheon without all ten churches deciding not to sponsor us."

Muttering words that burned Denni's ears and never failed to make her stomach churn, Leigh spun around and stomped out of the room.

The detective watched her go, his lips twisting into a sarcastic grin. "She's going to have to stop throwing herself at me. It's getting downright embarrassing."

Cate giggled. "It would definitely be a cold day—"

"Cate, will you please go up and let the other girls know we'll be starting on the basement soon?"

Denni shook her head. Living with a group of girls who held to no strong faith, and who had pretty much seen and heard it all, definitely presented its challenges. With the exception of Rissa, all of the girls attended services only as part of their requirement for living at Mahoney House. Rissa had found a true commitment to Christ last year.

Working to place children in foster homes for the past ten years, Denni had met caring families who provided loving, nurturing environments. The kids in those homes were the lucky ones. The children she was most concerned about were the others: the leftovers whose foster parents cashed the checks and spent them on their own pleasure, without providing properly for the children they had agreed to take in, the kids who fell through the cracks when they turned eighteen and the government stopped paying for their upkeep, at least as foster children. Many grew to adulthood and ended up in the welfare system, continuing a cycle of poverty and neglect.

Denni knew she couldn't fix the whole problem, but for five girls she was making a difference. At least she believed she was. Each was either in college or, in the case of Cate, taking online courses. Each had a part-time job as well and a mountain of hope for the future.

If she could pull off the luncheon Monday afternoon, perhaps there would be room for twenty more girls. Two houses, larger than the four-bedroom Victorian home she currently owned, each providing a home for ten, plus a house mother of sorts. Denni would then serve as a paid coordinator for all the houses.

She wanted it so badly she could taste it. Like a craving for milk chocolate or veal parmesan with sauce and gooey mozzarella cheese. It just had to be God's will.

"So, the girls…"

Detective Corrigan's voice brought her back to the

moment. The proverbial fly in the ointment. This guy's suspicions could blow everything sky-high. She had to find a way to convince him to point his investigation away from the girls.

Denni watched him as his gaze perused the five eight-by-ten photographs arranged on the mantel above the stone fireplace.

"What about the girls?" Defenses raised, Denni narrowed her gaze and geared up for a fight.

"They all look so innocent. You'd never know from these pictures that one of them could be responsible for the mishaps around here."

"They look innocent because they *are* innocent."

"We'll see."

"I don't understand why you're so sure one of my girls is responsible for these things, Reece. Again, what would they possibly have to gain?"

He lifted his eyebrow and she felt herself blush. "Detective Corrigan, I mean."

"Hey, don't worry about it. Reece is fine." He gave her a shiny, white-toothed grin. "And I'm not so sure it's one of them. Just checking out all of the possibilities. Denni."

She smiled back, trying to calm her racing pulse. "First-name basis, eh? Doesn't that seem a little friendly considering our positions? I shouldn't have initiated it."

"Maybe I like friendly." His eyes captured hers and held. Denni couldn't breathe. With every fiber of her being she wanted to believe that Reece truly found her appealing. But just as quickly, reason struck a dissonant chord and her chest tightened. He hadn't shown the slightest interest in her over the course of the three-month investigation, so why now? All of a sudden he was softening his stance about the girls. Pretending he wasn't so sure it was one of them when he'd never even considered anyone else before today.

She folded her arms. "All right, Corrigan. Just what are you trying to pull here?"

Reece couldn't help but grin at Denni, face twisted into a fierce scowl and her feet planted on the floor as though she were digging in for the fight of her life.

"I'm not trying to pull anything. Can't a guy think you're cute and want to get to know you better?" He gave her another smile and watched her closely, looking for a crack in her armor.

She sniffed. "Oh, sure. You think I'm a real cutie, don't you?" She shoved her hands onto her nicely rounded hips. "I'm exactly the same as I have been since you started slithering around here and you never looked twice before. As a matter of fact, I've recently put on about ten stress pounds. Real attractive, huh?"

Actually, it was. It gave her a softer, curvier look that kept him fighting to keep his eyes focused above her neck. This time he lost the battle and gave her a once-over. Three months of weekly or more visits had taken its toll on his reserve. Denni Mahoney was definitely under his skin.

She frowned and sent him a dismissive wave before he could voice his opinion. "It doesn't matter. I know what you're up to. Trying to get in on my good graces so that you have better access to the girls. Well, just forget it. And you know what? You can just leave." She pointed to the door.

Okay, so maybe he should have eased into the new strategy. Although, he did still have an ace in the hole. "I'm not going anywhere just yet."

"You are if I say so."

"I came here to pump out your basement, and I don't plan to leave until I do it."

"Because I'm so attractive you mean? You just can't help but be my knight in shining armor?"

Before he could answer, two of Denni's girls entered the room. Searching his memory, he drummed up their names. The tall one he knew was Shelley Bartlett, a brunette with wire-framed glasses and a minor slump in her shoulders that he imagined was due to her height. She stared at him then moved on, her expression softening as her gaze rested on Denni.

"Hey, Denni." Rissa Kelley practically bounced into the room. Plump and rosy-cheeked, she had a quick smile and a touch of a Southern drawl that was obviously put-on since he knew she'd lived her entire life in central Missouri. "Cate said we're ready to start cleaning up the basement."

"Just about." Denni looked past the girls toward the door. "Didn't Cate come back with you?"

"She started feeling a little dizzy," Leigh said, entering the room like a black cloud. Reece tensed. Was she going to explode into a vicious downpour? "I told her to stay in bed. She shouldn't be doing this kind of work, anyway."

Denni nodded. "Agreed. I'll check on her in a little while." She turned to Reece. "Are you ready to get started?"

"Isn't there one more of you?" Reece asked, determined not to be completely left out.

Leigh rolled her eyes. "How observant, Detective."

Oh, boy, would he like to slap the cuffs on that one and toss her into a cell. He'd lay odds she was behind this whole thing. Only, Denni had brought up a good point earlier. What was her motive? But he dismissed the thought. Not everyone needed a motive to try to harm the very people doing their best to help. Jonathon had been proof of that, hadn't he?

No one had seen the trouble beneath Jonathon's wall of pretense until the damage was done. And this Leigh Sommers had all the earmarks of making another Jonathon—a chip on her shoulder the size of Mount Rushmore, the black leather jacket, and an unconventional style that shouted rebellion. Oh, yeah. Leigh was trouble. Big trouble with a sweet smile beneath that street-smart exterior. She had the sort of smile that made a person want to give her the benefit of the doubt, encourage her to make good grades and earn her degree so she could rise above her upbringing.

But he knew better, and he would not be fooled again. "Forget it, Corrigan. I'm not interested in a bald, aging cop." Leigh's accusing tone shocked him to the present. He caught her glare and threw it right back.

"Believe me, trouble-making, body-pierced teens aren't exactly my type."

A deep blush appeared instantly on her cheeks. "I'm twenty-one," she muttered without making eye contact.

Feeling sufficiently back in control, Reece turned to Denni. "I asked about the other girl."

Denni brushed past him, headed toward the basement door. "Fran's showering. She's been out looking for work all day."

"I thought all the girls were already working."

"Fran is perpetually between jobs." Leigh rolled her eyes.

"Leigh!" Shelley glared at the other girl as if to say, "Don't diss one of our own in front of the *C-O-P*."

Reece gave her a lopsided grin. "Hey, don't worry about it. I won't automatically shoot her to the top of my suspect list just because she's jobless. It happens."

But he made a mental note. Someone without a steady income, "perpetually between jobs" rather, might just need to rip off her own benefactress for a little extra cash. Interesting new twist. Maybe he'd been concentrating on Leigh a little too much.

"You talking about me?" Fran entered the room, her face devoid of makeup. Wearing a blue T-shirt and ripped Levi's, she looked like a normal college student. But then looks were deceiving.

"Well, Detective, if you seriously want to help us, then I suggest we get started pumping out the water." Skepticism sparked in Denni's eyes as though she knew full well what the news of Fran's employment status had done to his list of suspects.

He winked at her and she blushed.

Inwardly he acknowledged that blush for what it was. She might not be a pushover for a compliment, but she was a woman. And it was becoming more evident that she was just as attracted to him as he was to her. He didn't like the thought of using her feelings against her. But after months of a cold investigation, it might just be time to mix things up.

Chapter Three

❧

With a gasp, Denni snatched up her soggy scrapbook from the drying floor. Her heart twisted inside her chest and she captured her bottom lip between her teeth.

How could she have been stupid enough to leave her cherished baby book downstairs? One rule of the house was to put things back where they belonged. Too bad she hadn't followed her own stinking directive. She hadn't even thought to look for it when she'd first seen the flood.

Her mother had faithfully contributed to the baby book filled with childhood highlights that extended to Denni's graduation day. She'd presented the book with a red ribbon tied around it the day Denni left for college.

Denni lifted a loose photograph next to where the book had lain. She picked it up. Her favorite picture of Mom and her. Denni had been three years old and mom was swinging her around the room. Mom's ringing laughter was almost audible through the picture.

Mom had been like that. All fun and surprises and full of hugs and warmth. That first day of adulthood for

Denni had been the last time she'd seen her mother alive. Two months later, the most important woman in Denni's life had collided with a drunk driver and had instantly gone to be with Jesus. And now the photo was ruined, half the ink washed away.

"You planning to eat supper?"

Yanked from the memory of her mother's face, Denni turned toward the steps, following the sound of Reece's voice. She squared her shoulders and forced control.

"I came down to see if you're going to have pizza. Those girls can pack it away like a high-school football team. If you don't hurry, you'll be out of luck."

Discovering her most cherished possession soaked and ruined had effectively robbed Denni of her appetite. She shrugged.

"They can have it. I'll grab something later if I'm hungry."

He walked toward her, his boots squishing on the puddled concrete. "Hey, you okay?" He glanced down at the book in her hand and his face sobered. "Special memories?"

Not trusting herself to speak, she nodded.

"Maybe you can salvage some of it."

Tears sprang to her eyes, a knee-jerk reaction to a sympathetic tone and his warm, gentle touch on her shoulder.

"Let me take a look at it," he said softly. "You know men are the problem solvers of the world." He gave her a lopsided grin.

Gratefully, she surrendered her book and the ruined photograph, hoping against hope that he'd give her the solution her muddled brain couldn't seem to form. She honestly didn't know if he was putting her on or not with that boyish grin, but if he could figure out a way to save her keepsakes, she was willing to give him the benefit of the doubt.

He carried the book across the room and set it on top of her laundry table. Carefully, he opened the cover. He smiled.

"This is you?"

She nodded.

"Cute."

Rolling her eyes, she stepped away. "Thanks." She enjoyed the way he handled her memories with gentle care, his long fingers working open the damaged pages.

"These pages are removable," he said. "If we take them out and spread them on the table to dry, you should be able to salvage most of the album. They won't be like they were before, but at least you'll still have your special memories."

"It's sweet of you to try to help."

"It means a lot to you, huh?"

"Everyone treasures their baby book."

"Not everyone has one."

Something in his voice alerted her instincts. She set aside the first baby page then angled her head to meet his gaze. Her breath caught. Raw pain flashed through his eyes, instantly, briefly, and then it was gone. But she'd seen it. Had caught him unawares. She suddenly wanted to discover what made this man tick.

"Want to talk about it?"

He gave a short laugh. "About what? Not having a baby book?"

She shrugged "It obviously bothers you."

"Honey, you have a lot to learn about men." That condescending tone caused her to clench her fists and fight to keep from socking him. It made her feel foolish. And she didn't like that feeling. Especially since he was right. What did she know about men? She'd never had a long-standing boyfriend and had only gone on a few dates. Still, he didn't have to be so hateful.

With a sniff she turned back to her salvaging efforts. "And you have a lot to learn about being nice to someone who wants to help."

He drew a ragged breath, but she refused to look again. Let him wallow in his childhood pain. She wouldn't be his punching bag.

"Hey." His fingers touched her shoulder, brushing back an errant strand of hair that had escaped her ponytail.

"What?"

His lips curved upward into a smile. "I'm a jerk."

Searching his slightly self-mocking smile, she rolled her eyes and nudged him with her shoulder. "So tell me something I don't already know."

A chuckle rumbled low in his chest. "Forgive me?"

"Sure, Corrigan."

Amid the whirring of the fans and dehumidifiers, they stood side by side saving Denni's memories.

Reece couldn't help but feel that he was invading a very private part of Denni's life as he dabbed page after page of her baby book and set them aside to continue drying. He felt, rather than saw, her chest rise as she took a shuddering breath. He glanced at the page she held. On it, a photograph of a little girl holding a baby. The handwritten caption beneath read: Denni, Always The Little Mother.

"That was me. Always mothering anyone or anything that would let me." She pronounced the statement as though not really speaking to him.

"Who's the baby?"

She jerked her gaze to his. "What? Oh." A smile tipped the corners of her lips. "My little sister, Keri. She just got married a few weeks ago. Guess who was her maid of honor?"

"I'm sure you looked better than the bride. The bridesmaids always do."

She scowled and Reece could have kicked himself. "Yeah, well. That's never been my experience. Believe me. And yes, I've been a bridesmaid more than twice— four times if you really want to know—and you know what that means."

Could he ever say the right thing? He glanced back at the page and sought to get her mind off the whole "three times a bridesmaid never a bride" scenario. "So you always played the little mother, eh?"

A sigh left her and she set the page down on the table. "Yeah. I have two sisters. Keri and an older sister named Raven. I'll probably be her bridesmaid too if she ever stops yanking around on guys' hearts long enough to fall in love."

"Tell me about your sisters." Instinctively, he knew it was the right move, knew that she needed to get something off her chest, not to mention her need to stop thinking about weddings.

"Raven takes after our mom. Free-spirited, independent, a real heartbreaker." She lifted a page from the table. "This is her on my graduation day."

"Pretty."

"That's putting it mildly. Raven was and still is the beauty of the family. Keri was the cute-as-a-button baby. I was…well…I was the bossy one." She gave a short laugh. "Mom always said I was born in the wrong order."

"Why's that?"

"You know. The oldest is supposed to be the bossy, controlling one. Raven just wanted to be left alone to do her own thing. Still does." She cut her glance to him. "Where are you in the family line?"

Expelling a short laugh, Reece spoke before he thought.

"Which one?"

"Which one what?"

A sudden image of family after family flashed across his mind like a slide show, blinking faster and faster until all of the different foster mothers and fathers and foster brothers and sisters jumbled together into one enormous group. Then they vanished and in their place one terrifying image remained. Jonathon. Standing over the only two people Reece had ever felt truly loved him. The teen's eyes had been more wild than ever that night as he looked at Reece. "I told you, man. I told you I was going to do it."

Thomas and Lydia Ide. The only two grownups he'd ever loved. He'd called them Mom and Dad in his mind but had never given in and said it aloud. He regretted that now. It would have meant so much to Mom.

His throat constricted. He coughed into his fist, trying to ease the ache.

"It's getting late. I'll be back in the morning to help move the furniture outside. It's supposed to be sunny all day tomorrow. If everyone pitches in, you should be ready for lunch guests on Monday."

Her soft brown eyes clouded in disappointment. She squared her shoulders and respected his need to change the subject. "I appreciate all you did today, Reece. I don't know what I'd have done without you."

Reece nodded, but turned away. He didn't want to be

drawn in by soft sentiments. There were too many emotions bombarding him at the moment as it was. The objective was to gain her trust, not lose his heart.

Denni heard the door open slowly then click shut. She glanced at the digital readout on the clock next to her bed and sighed—12:18 a.m. Fran again.

Closing her book, she set it aside and pushed back the quilt. She walked down the steps, the soft glow from the kitchen alerting her to Fran's whereabouts.

The muted sound of the refrigerator shutting made her smile. It reminded her of nights when she and her sisters would come in after dates. There was always an ice-cream powwow around the table.

She stepped into the kitchen. "So, you waited up just like a mommy, huh?"

Reality crashed the party in the form of Fran's sarcastic tone. Her tiny frame leaned against the counter. She munched on a slice of leftover pizza, and sipped a can of cola.

"Not exactly like a mother," Denni said, not allowing her tone to betray her irritation. "More like a concerned friend."

A short laugh from the girl brought a frown to Denni's brow. "What's bothering you, Fran?"

"Nothing." She gulped the drink, glaring over the aluminum rim. "I just don't know why you treat us like we're fourteen years old. That's all. I swear it's almost as bad as that bat next door peeping out of her window at us every time we make a move. Like we're always doing something wrong, or something."

"I don't necessarily think you're doing something wrong, but you know the rules of the house." Denni observed the blond-headed girl. Gorgeous enough to have been a model if not for the perpetual sneer on her face. "You didn't say goodbye after dinner. I was worried."

"Worried? About me, or worried that I won't find a job? If all your girls aren't productive contributors to the betterment of our great society, you might be considered a failure."

Taken aback, Denni grabbed a paper plate from the cabinet and helped herself to a slice of pizza to distract herself from the sudden hurt. "Come and sit with me, okay? Let's talk about this."

Fran's expression softened, but she gave a careless shrug. "Whatever."

"How was your day? We didn't have a chance to talk earlier, what with cleaning the basement." Denni would have to deal with the girl's failure to make curfew, but not now. Not when Fran was on the defensive.

"I didn't find a job if that's what you're asking." She slouched in the seat, propping her feet on the chair catty-cornered from her.

"I wasn't asking."

Obviously, something—or someone—had slapped a huge chip on her shoulder today and she was raring for a fight. Denni refused to play into it.

"I looked for one. Jobs just aren't so easy to find when you don't have a degree."

"I know. I could try to help you if you want me to."

In a flash, Fran shoved up from her chair, tipping it. It crashed to the floor. Anger flashed in her eyes as she faced Denni. "Would you get off my back? I said I'd find something."

Stay calm. Don't kick her out just because she's made you uncomfortable.

Scared was more like it. Fran had exhibited a violent side more than once. But the tendency had never been directed at Denni or any of the girls as far as Denni knew. Slow-moving traffic, barking dogs, inattentive waitresses. All had suffered Fran's sharp tongue.

Denni stood and faced the shaking girl. "Fran, I know you're trying to get a job, and I understand how frustrating it is that you can't find anything. But I can't allow you to treat me this way."

"What are you going to do, kick me out?" The girl persisted in her bravado, but Denni saw the slight tremble of her lip.

Thank you for letting me see that, Lord.

Without it, Denni probably would have asked her to find another place to live. Instead she stepped forward and lightly gripped Fran by her upper arms. "No, I am not going to kick you out. Everyone deserves a second chance."

Mouth agape, Fran stared through unbelievably blue eyes. "You're kidding me."

Denni shook her head. "Of course I'm not, but we have to reestablish the rules first."

Fran rolled her eyes. "Figures."

"Especially when someone is obviously trying to hurt us, or scare us off, Fran. I want to know you girls are safe."

"I can take care of myself," she muttered.

Clamping her lips tightly, Denni dropped her hands from Fran's arms. "I don't doubt your abilities to handle yourself, but the rules exist for a reason and everyone abides by them. When you're not going to be home by curfew you have to call and let us know where you are, who you're with and how close to being home you are at the moment. Working late is the only exception to that rule."

As if by divine emphasis, the lock rattled and the front door opened. A second later, Leigh came into the kitchen. Just after Reece had gone home earlier, Leigh had been called in to cover another girl's shift at the barbecue shack where she waited tables.

"What are you two doing up so late?"

"Getting lectured," Fran groused.

"I'm sure you deserve it." Leigh smiled to remove the sting, but Denni could see in the hardness of her eyes that she meant it. Leigh worked hard at school and at work. Her payoff was a 4.0 average and a boss who begged her to take on a management role at the restaurant. But Leigh wanted none of it. She was going to be a physical therapist and she didn't need to be tied down to extra responsibilities and more hours at work.

Denni could see attitude sweep over Fran, but the girl knew better than to tangle with Leigh. Abandoned before the age of ten to the streets, Leigh had survived until a police officer found her hooking at the age of fourteen. The girl knew how to take care of herself.

"We'll finish this in the morning," Denni said.

Fran nodded and stomped from the kitchen. Denni watched her go, wishing she knew what to say to make her understand that the world was not out to get her.

"Sheesh, what's her problem this time?" At Leigh's irritated tone, Denni turned back to face her.

"She missed curfew."

"What's with the chair knocked over? Did she threaten you?" Leigh's eyes narrowed to angry slits. "Denni, tell me the truth."

Denni walked to the chair and righted it. "Of course

not. She just stood up too fast and the chair fell over." Which was true of only the barest description of the event.

Obviously not buying it, Leigh shook her head. "If she ever threatens you, tell me. I'll make sure she never does it again."

A warmth filled Denni at Leigh's fierce loyalty. "Thanks, Leigh. But trust me when I tell you Fran wouldn't hurt me. She just overreacts." She grinned. "Like someone else I know."

Leigh chuckled and slid her arm around Denni's shoulders. "You gave us all a chance to make something of our lives. I'm grateful. And no one is going to hurt you while I have anything to say about it."

Slipping her arm around the girl's slender waist, Denni gave her a little squeeze then let her go. "I'm going to wipe down the counters and table before I go to bed. But you go on up. I know you're exhausted."

A yawn stretched Leigh's mouth at the suggestion. "You're right. I'm going to bed. Corrigan coming tomorrow?" She said it like the name caused a bitter taste in her mouth.

"Yes. He'll be here early with some of his friends to move the furniture outside so it can dry and air out."

"Well, maybe he'll be good for something after all." She stopped. "You're not by any chance falling for this guy, are you?"

Heat crept to Denni's cheeks. "You don't have to worry. Detective Corrigan doesn't have any interest in me beyond this case."

A dubious half smile lifted one corner of Leigh's lips. "Yeah, right." She opened her mouth as if to comment further, but stopped and cocked her head. She frowned. "Do you hear that?"

"What?" But she did hear it…water running through the pipes. As if… Denni's heart nearly beat from her chest. "Not again!" Leigh outran her to the basement door. She flew down the steps.

"It's coming in again!"

Without waiting for an answer, Denni sped through the kitchen to the back door and outside. The water was running full force. With a frustrated cry, she twisted the handle until the water trickled, dripped, then stopped. She dropped to her knees on the ground, tears of anger streaming down her face. Leigh reached her and stood over her, hands on hips, her chest heaving.

Denni moaned. "Why would anyone want to stop this project? Why?"

"I don't know, Denni. But not much water got in this time. We can use the shopvac to get rid of it. Obviously whoever turned it on didn't expect us to hear it so soon." Leigh squatted down and began twisting the handle.

"What are you doing?"

"Taking this off. I don't know why I didn't think about it before."

"Good idea."

They returned to the house and Leigh dropped the handle into the junk drawer. "Well, I'm going to bed." She gave Denni a quick hug. "Don't worry. The basement is officially off-limits to anyone trying to cause damage."

Denni nodded. "'Night."

She double-checked the doors to make sure they were all locked, then headed to bed. Staring up at the dark ceiling, Denni went back over the events of the night. What if Reece was right? Had Fran turned on the faucet before coming inside? Maybe that's why she'd been so defensive. Or… Denni cringed at the very thought. What if Leigh hadn't really heard the water? What if she'd actually just known the water was running? After all, Denni hadn't heard it the entire time she and Fran had been sitting in the kitchen. How had Leigh?

Her chest tightened and she sat up, swinging her legs over the side of the bed. She tiptoed across the room and back down the stairs. In the kitchen, she slid open the junk drawer and lifted out the faucet handle. Back in her bedroom, she twisted the lock on her bedroom door—the first time she'd locked it in the two years since opening the house. With the cold handle still in her hand, she headed back to her bed. She stared at it for a long time. Imagining five scenarios. Each girl creeping into the night and turning on the water. With a shudder, she placed the handle in her bedside drawer and settled back against her pillow.

She closed her eyes, but sleep refused to come. For the first time in the three months since the first mishap, she was beginning to wonder…was Reece right? Was one of her girls out to cause her harm?

Chapter Four

Reece stared at his forty-inch, flat-screen TV—a perk that went along with being a thirty-five-year-old law-enforcement officer with no responsibilities to anyone but himself. Not that he had much time to watch the thing. Monday was his day to eat a home-cooked meal—even though he was the one to cook it—and catch up on a week's worth of recorded TV shows.

Today, however, the efforts of a half-dozen sunburned, undernourished millionaire-wannabes failed to keep his attention and his mind drifted miles away from the so-called reality show playing out before him.

The memory of Denni's neighbor tossed back and forth in his brain. He hadn't even asked her name. What kind of a cop was he anyway?

Could the old lady have sabotaged Mahoney House? She certainly had motive, since she'd made no secret of her objection to the girls living in her neighborhood. But what about the thefts? Theoretically, he supposed, it was possible for her to have sneaked into the house and lifted the items. Especially if she had an accomplice. But

45

why would the obviously well-to-do lady steal? Just to
scare Denni and the girls away?

A vigorous rub of his sleek, shaved head did nothing to alleviate the frustration at his inability to put two
and two together. Times like these were rare. He could
count on one hand the number of cases he'd failed to
crack in his past fifteen years on the force. And despite
the fact that he had the best record of any of his fellow
officers by a long shot, he still didn't like the math.
Failure wasn't in his vocabulary.

To make matters worse, his captain had been asking
questions about the Mahoney case lately—enough that
Reece was beginning to avoid the guy. After three
months, the captain was getting close to filing the case
in the back of the cabinet and assigning Reece another
one. He hadn't said as much, but Reece could read him
like a book, and his stomach sank with dread every time
they made eye contact.

If Denni had reported the basement-flooding incident
it might have given oomph to the case and roused the
captain's interest again. As it was, Reece knew his days
on the Mahoney investigation were numbered—at least
in an official capacity.

A sense of urgency nipped his insides, and he shifted
in his overstuffed recliner. He conjured the image of the
auburn-haired Denni. She didn't deserve to have her
dream snuffed out. He'd never known anyone quite like
her before and he had to admit that at least fifty percent
of his reason for wanting to solve the case was because
he was tired of seeing the two lines of worry creasing
her brow just above her perky little nose. A smile touched
his lips. Obeying impulse, he reached for the phone and
lifted the receiver. He dialed her number by heart.

One ring, two… He frowned at three, and growled at four, and was just about to hang up when a breathless voice filtered through the wires. "Hello?"

"Denni? What's wrong?"

"Reece?"

"Yeah." Just the sound of her voice raised his heart rate. "Everything okay?"

"No. Everything is just rotten!"

Her emphatic response took him aback. He raised his eyebrows. "Another incident?" This time he would definitely check the neighbor lady's whereabouts.

"Not like that." She didn't even try to hide her irritation, and that irritated him. "Why are you so suspicious all the time?"

Okay, he hadn't expected to get barked at. "Because I'm a cop. And because there's an ongoing investigation surrounding you."

"Well, this has nothing to do with your investigation. I just spoke to my caterer, who should have been here setting up about a half hour ago. Only, *she* insists the luncheon was cancelled. Which of course is ridiculous, because why on earth would I cancel the most important lunch of my life? Regardless, she has nothing she can prepare on a moment's notice, so I have nothing to feed the ten people who could be deciding the future of Mahoney project."

Her voice caught, halting her rant, and Reece stopped breathing as the hero in him rose to the surface.

"What are you going to do?"

"I don't really have a choice. Cancel." Defeat and tears mingled in her voice.

Reece kicked down the footrest on the recliner and grabbed for his brown leather sandals. "Get the dining room all set up. Don't worry about the food. I'll be there in forty-five minutes."

"Forty-five minutes? Reece, do you realize the luncheon is in exactly—oh, good grief—two hours and fifty-four minutes."

"Have a little faith, woman. And trust me."

Denni watched, fascinated and eternally grateful, as Reece slid another grilled chicken breast from the indoor grill. Dressed in a pair of baggy jean shorts and a T-shirt, sleeves rolled up and straining over bulging sun-bronzed biceps, he was way too distracting on a day when she needed all of her wits about her. On the other hand, if his distracting personage hadn't shown up bearing three bags of groceries, she'd be sunk.

"Hey, you going to slice those peppers? I need to get them on the grill."

Denni jumped at the sound of Reece's slightly urgent tone. "Sorry," she muttered and turned her attention back to the task she'd been assigned by the chef: slicing red bell peppers to add to the mix. She had to admit the guy had saved the day. Grilled chicken wraps on whole-wheat tortillas and a large Caesar salad made a perfect luncheon. It spoke of class, but didn't look like she was trying too hard. And best of all, the entire meal would be ready in less than an hour, and she would still have time for a quick shower before the guests began arriving. The girls had pitched in and prepared iced tea, coffee and strawberry shortcakes for dessert.

The thought of their worry when she'd made the wretched announcement of the caterer's incompetence sent affection surging through her. And she felt guilty for ever entertaining the notion that one of them might be out to close her down. She'd have to be careful from now on not to let herself be drawn into Reece's world of suspicion.

"All done," she announced, scooping up the sliced peppers and tossing them into a bowl. She walked across to the other counter where the grill sat. Intent on cubing the chicken, Reece looked up only briefly, as she set the bowl on the counter, but in that instant, he sent her a knee-weakening smile.

"Thanks," he said.

"You're welcome." Oh, be still my beating heart, she pleaded.

"Why don't you go get yourself ready?" he suggested. "I can finish up here. By the time you come back, I'll have everything cleaned up and you'll be all set to wow the powers that be."

Could this guy possibly be the same man who had breezed in and out of her life at irregular times over the past three months? He couldn't. But she could definitely get used to this Reece Corrigan. A simple thank-you just didn't seem appropriate at a time like this. Still, she had to say something. "Reece, I don't know what I would have done without you today. I'll find a way to repay you."

He shrugged. "It was only around fifty dollars. Consider it my contribution to your life's ambition."

Fifty dollars! She'd forgotten about the grocery bill! "For crying out loud, why didn't you say something? Let me get my purse." She reached for her bag, which remained on the counter where she'd set it earlier when she'd frantically searched for the caterer's card. That moment of panic seemed a million years ago, now that all was well.

Reece caught hold of her wrist. "Forget it. I wanted to do it."

"But why?"

His gaze locked with hers, and the honesty in his eyes melted away the periphery until he was all she saw. "Let's not analyze it," he said softly.

Denni nodded, swallowing hard. Reece released her wrist and jerked his head toward the doorway. "Now go, make yourself presentable." He turned back to the meal preparation, obviously finished with any discussion.

There was nothing for her to do but follow his instructions. At the door, she turned. "You will stay for lunch, won't you?" It was the least she could do, she silently admonished herself. To allow him to save the day and then not even bother to invite him to join them would have been plain rude. And her mother hadn't raised her to be ill-mannered.

"I'm not exactly dressed for a luncheon," he said.

"I disagree. No one specified dressy." By the dubious look on his face, she knew he wasn't buying it. Everyone would be dressed in suits or other professional clothes. As a matter of fact, she'd intended to dress professionally herself, but if it would make him feel more comfortable...

"Dress appropriately, Denni," he said as though reading her thoughts. "I don't need to stay for lunch."

She hesitated, wanting to insist, but afraid she'd sound needy and desperate. A single thirty-something woman clinging to the man who had come to her rescue. But she did want to prolong his presence. She couldn't help it.

"I'll call later to see how everything turns out."

Denni's eyes grew wide at his knowing smile. Had

she said that thing about wanting to prolong his presence aloud? Well, she couldn't have him thinking she wanted him to stick around because of some personal attachment or crush or something. So she did all she knew to do. Gave a shrug. "Whatever. Just don't forget to take your grill home."

He chuckled. "I won't."

She hurried up the stairs to the solace of the bathroom where she could soak away her humiliation and be alone with her confusing emotions, which seemed increasingly to be favoring Reece Corrigan.

Reece was just drying the last of the mixing bowls, knives and cutting boards and putting them into the cabinets when the doorbell rang. He looked around. The women of the house had adjourned upstairs, presumably to get ready for the luncheon. Personally, Reece thought it was risky on Denni's part to include the pregnant Cate, the body-pierced, tattooed Leigh and the explosive Fran, but no one had asked his opinion, and he knew offering it to Denni would only undo the good he'd done by making his famous grilled chicken wraps and saving Denni's behind for the day.

The bell chimed again and Leigh called down, "Corrigan, get the door, already. Can't you see we're busy? Or do you want us to come down in our skivvies?"

He was almost sure he heard *idiot* added, but had no solid proof.

He put on his best smile and opened the door. Four professionally dressed people stood on the porch. One woman, dressed in a navy-blue suit and three men, similarly clad. They gave him the once-over, setting his defenses on edge. Couldn't a guy wear a pair of shorts during his time off?

"I'm afraid we must have the wrong address," the tallish woman said. "We're looking for Miss Mahoney?"

"Yeah, she's taking a shower." Immediately he regretted giving into his wicked side—the side of him that loved to shock women like this piece of work standing in front of him.

"And you are…?"

"Oh, excuse me…" He wiped his hands on his apron—oh, brother, he was still wearing the apron—and offered his hand. "Detective Corrigan. I'm a friend of Denni's." He stepped aside. "Won't you come in?"

With quadruple curt nods, they stepped inside, each set of eyes darting around the living room, beginning their perusal before they even got comfortable.

The doorbell chimed again, and Reece mentally prepared himself for another once-over. This time, however, Denni showed up, her disturbing floral scent breezing into the room ahead of her. "Oh, good, you've all met Reece." She turned to him. "Would you please get the door while I show these guests to the dining room?"

Suddenly wishing for a three-piece suit, Reece realized he was staying for lunch.

Chapter Five

Denni barely touched her lunch. Not that she didn't try. Every time she brought the wrap to her mouth, someone asked another question. Finally, she gave up and sipped her iced tea instead. Just as well, she conceded. Her tied-in-knots stomach probably would have rejected any intruders anyway.

The girls, seated amongst the guests, were thankfully on their best behavior—including Fran and Leigh—who had settled into a fragile peace after the tension of the other night.

The nine male liaisons present seemed amiable enough, genuinely interested in the mission. Denni smiled as Mr. Terrie, representing one of the smaller churches, patted his lips with his napkin and addressed her. "This is a unique idea, Miss Mahoney. Intriguing. I can't help but be impressed with the desire to provide training and guidance to girls who have grown up in foster care."

Under the table, Reece nudged her knee with his. She turned to him and he winked. A flush crept to her cheeks and she averted her gaze quickly. "Thank you, Mr. Terrie. I feel as if this is a God idea."

"What I must question," broke in Elizabeth Wilson, AKA Cruella DeVille, "Is whether or not it is really necessary to take care of legally adult individuals. Isn't that what the welfare system is for? Perhaps our funds would be better spent elsewhere."

Leigh's eyes flashed across from Denni, but to her credit she kept her mouth shut. Denni fought to maintain a pleasant expression. "The welfare system is for adults who need help…yes. But statistically, once an individual becomes dependent on the state, it's almost impossible for them to break free, particularly if they become pregnant out of wedlock. After bearing three or four children, these young women are trapped for life and rearing children who are, themselves, in danger of repeating the cycle of foster care and adult dependency on welfare."

"But surely not in every case," Elizabeth Wilson challenged. Her cold gaze swept the girls. "Do you feel you'd end up on welfare if not for Miss Mahoney's charity?"

Denni bristled. And before she could respond, a knowing sense of dread shifted through her and from the corner of her eye, she saw Fran rise to her feet.

"Lady, are you trying to imply we're all a bunch of charity cases?" Red splotches of rage popped out on Fran's face and neck.

"Aren't you?"

"We work and contribute to the household."

"Really?"

Denni cringed at what she sensed was about to come.

"And where *do* you work?" Elizabeth asked, her lips

twisting into what Denni could have sworn was a smug smile, as though she knew the answer to the question before she ever asked. Pity welled up in Denni's heart as Fran sputtered. "Well, I…I'm trying to find a job."

"I see…"

"I don't think you do see, Miss Wilson." Leigh leaned forward in her chair and fixed the pinched old maid with an intimidating glare. "Fran is right. We all work to pay our way here. Fran is pounding the pavement every day trying to find a job. We're a family and we'll stay together even if it means you and your kind can't find it in your hearts to see the merits of this sort of program."

Pounding the pavement was a bit of a stretch, but maternal pride at Leigh's loyalty to her "sister" nearly caused tears to rise to the surface. Denni held them in check.

"Are there any other questions before we begin the tour?" Denni asked, deliberately focusing her attention away from Elizabeth. She breathed a heavy sigh when the woman fixed her gaze on Cate. The sweet girl grew red and placed a protective hand over her growing belly.

"What would be the screening process to determine who is allowed to live in the centers?"

"First of all. These are homes, not centers," Denni replied. "Second of all, the only criteria I find necessary other than the obvious one of being out of the foster-care system and in need of mentoring, is that the girls be willing either to work full-time or go to school."

"Surely you aren't suggesting college?"

Leigh was bristling again, and Denni spoke up swiftly. "As a matter of fact, all five of my girls are in school and doing a great job."

Elizabeth's brow rose and her gaze darted once more to Cate's stomach.

"Cate takes classes over the Internet," Denni said, smiling broadly at the girl. "Next year she'll register for classes at the university."

"And how will she pay for these classes? Will part of the funding you're requesting go toward that?"

"No." As far as Denni was concerned, this was the first reasonable question Elizabeth had asked so far. "Our Cate received a scholarship that will cover all expenses, including books. And for the others, there are also scholarships or government grants, and if necessary, student loans. These girls want it badly enough that nothing will stop them from getting an education."

Elizabeth nodded, but her gaze hadn't left Cate. "I assume the child will be placed with a family?"

Cate frowned and shook her head. "I'm keeping my baby."

"Do you think that's wise? How will you take care of a baby when you need someone else to take care of you?"

It was a deliberate jab, and Denni felt like decking the nasty woman. How could anyone call themselves a Christian and be so mean?

Mr. Terrie cleared his throat. "We are not here to judge the girls, Miss Wilson. I'm sure you'll agree that society does enough of that."

Denni could have hugged him on the spot.

Mr. Clark, who had stuffed himself with three chicken wraps and avoided the entire unpleasant scene, now came up for air. "These are wonderful."

"Thank you." Denni couldn't resist a grin and a nudge on Reece's arm. "But you should be complimenting our cook. The detective, here, saved the day when the caterer failed to show up."

"Fabulous." The pudgy liaison kissed the tips of his fingers Italian-style.

"Thanks," Reece said. "It was my honor to rescue a damsel in distress.

Leigh snorted and muttered under her breath. Reece's brows narrowed in obvious anticipation as he waited for her to take the offensive in a verbal battle. Denni breathed a silent prayer that Leigh would just for once keep it together where Reece was concerned.

The girl cleared her throat and plucked at her napkin, clearly willing to save her barb for another day.

"I can't imagine the caterer not showing up. Didn't you cancel?"

Surprise lifted Denni's brows at Elizabeth's question. "No, we didn't. But coincidentally, that's exactly what the caterer claims happened."

"How did you know about it?" Reece asked sharply.

For the first time, Elizabeth's composure faltered. "I just…Linda is my sister."

Reece scowled. "Linda?"

"The caterer," Denni murmured. "I see. You thought the luncheon had been cancelled, according to your sister, but you showed up anyway?"

"I—" She shrugged. "I suppose so."

Reece opened his mouth to speak again, but Denni sent a hard kick in his direction, hoping to make contact beneath the table. A pained expression covered his face, and he snapped his mouth shut as he clearly got the message.

Now was not the time for Reece to give in to his cop nature and start interrogating her guests. The guy had all the instincts of a guppy. How he'd ever made it on the police force this long was a mystery to her.

Elizabeth…

Of course. The woman had once been turned down as a potential foster parent because of a felony drug conviction. Denni had been the one to break the news. And Elizabeth had been furious, had insisted the arrest had been a mistake. But that was five years ago. They'd seen each other at church since then, and Elizabeth had always been cordial. Surely she couldn't be holding a grudge…

Oh, criminy. I'm getting as suspicious as Reece.

She glanced up to find Elizabeth looking at her, resentment marring her features. "I believe we're ready for the tour now, Miss Mahoney. If we dare tour an all-female house." Mr. Terrie's teasing grin and fatherly tone effectively smoothed out the rough tension that seemed to have everyone on edge.

He placed an arm about Cate's shoulders. Fear sprang to the girl's eyes, and Denni held her breath.

"When is the blessed event to take place, young lady?" he asked.

A tentative smile touched Cate's lips as he dropped his arm as though nothing were amiss, but Denni knew he had to sense Cate's resistance. "In about a month."

"Parenting is the most precious gift God granted to his human creation," he said. "He'll guide you as you raise this child up to love Him."

Elizabeth clamped her lips together and brushed past the rest of the group.

Tears welled in Cate's eyes. "Thank you," she whispered.

Denni sent a silent praise heavenward. Sweet, sweet Cate. You see? Not all men are out to hurt you. A lump formed in her throat as she followed the group, while the girls led the way through the dining room into the kitchen where they had agreed they would begin the tour.

A warm hand wrapped hers and she looked up, immediately captured by Reece's gentle gaze. He leaned in close to her ear. "You handled the luncheon superbly. The men were eating out of your hand. You have nothing to worry about."

Joy rose inside her, but crashed before reaching her lips as Mr. Jordan's voice carried through the kitchen from the deck just outside. "There may be a bit of a problem, Miss Mahoney."

Denni closed the door behind the last guest. She plopped onto the large rust-colored sofa with a defeated groan. "There's no way I can get all those things fixed within a month."

Reece's heart went out to her. After facing down Elizabeth and pretty much overpowering her objections, to have structural and repair problems crop up and threaten to keep the sponsors from committing just seemed cruel.

"You're in luck."

Leigh turned to him, not bothering to mask her contempt. "Are you hallucinating again, Corrigan? How can you get luck out of rotten boards and bad plumbing?"

Reece returned Leigh's glare. Apparently the brief truce was over. But that was okay. Let the little twerp insult him. One look at the pained expression on Denni's face and his mind was made up. No more arguing with the girls. He was taking the high road on this one.

"It just so happens that I work with a group of amateur carpenters and plumbers." Most of the guys on his shift were married with families and tinkered around their houses on their days off. They'd love the chance to try out their tool belts. The ones their wives tried to hide just before calling professionals to take care of household repairs.

"How about it?"

Denni's brow furrowed and the right side of her bottom lip disappeared between her teeth. "I don't know…"

Reece drew a sharp breath at the longing filling him. When had he become so chivalrous? As a cop, he was sworn to serve and protect, but he'd never had the impulse to protect and serve one single woman before.

"What you're trying to do here is important, Denni. If you succeed with only one out of these five girls, it will make our job easier. Make society better by one person becoming educated and stopping the cycle. So consider it our contribution."

Leigh snorted and, this time, didn't hold back her retort as she had during lunch. "If you want to make a contribution, how about giving us the cash to get someone out here who knows what he's doing?"

"Leigh!" Denni's face glowed with embarrassment, as though Leigh's rudeness was somehow her fault.

"It's all right. Leigh's got a point. I could pay for part of the repairs, or I could spend that money on supplies and get all the repairs finished." He gave Leigh a look that caused her nose ring to move with her flared nostrils. "What do you think would be the smartest course of action?"

She shrugged. "Twist it all you want, Corrigan. But we both know you're not doing this for the betterment of society or to help the needy. You're just trying to find evidence to pin on one of us."

"You scared?" Reece shot back, rattled by her astute accusation and forgetting his resolve to take the "high road."

A sneer marred her face. "Of you? Not in a million years." She glanced at Denni. "I have to get ready for work." Without another word, she stormed out of the room.

"Well, I think it's a fantastic idea," Fran offered.

Reece figured her opinion was more a desire to take the opposite position from Leigh. Still, he pounced on the fragile support. "You see? That's one of your girls with a little common sense. What about the rest of you?"

"I think it's a good idea, too," Cate said timidly. "We really can't afford it otherwise, even if everyone pitches in extra. And it's not like any of us are really around much anyway, so he can't bug us that much. So I vote yes."

Reece smirked "All right. That's two votes yes, one vote no."

"I'm with Leigh." Shelley walked to the couch and sat next to Denni. "Don't let him fool you, Denni. He's playing you just to get information. First he fixes lunch, now he wants to fix the house? Why this sudden interest? Huh? Leigh's right. He's just trying to get something on us."

"So…that's two and two," Reece said, deliberately choosing not to respond to Shelley's accusation, which was only partly true.

Holding his breath, he looked at Rissa, the tie-breaker. "Well," the chubby faux-Southern belle said, a twinkle lighting her eyes, "I think it's a marvelous idea."

"Well, we've never voted on anything before." Shelley's biting tone shot down Reece's optimism. "It's Denni's decision, anyway, not ours."

Denni looked at the girls. "No. Shelley, you're wrong. This is a decision we all have to make. This is a good thing. I'm adding my vote to Fran, Cate and Rissa. I can't think of a solid reason to refuse Reece's offer."

"How about the fact that he thinks one of us ripped you off and flooded the basement?"

Denni took Shelley's hand, but her eyes were fixed on Reece and he got the message loud and clear, even before she spoke.

"No one here has anything to hide, so if Detective Corrigan is just trying to weasel his way into our lives in order to find something to incriminate one of you, he's going to be working hard to repair the deck and the plumbing for no reason."

Rissa let out a giggle. "And it would serve you right."

Reece couldn't resist a grin. He had to admit, the drawl was growing on him more each time Rissa turned her friendly smile in his direction.

"So, it's settled then?"

"Whatever." Shelley pushed up from the couch and followed Leigh's example, stomping from the room.

"We accept your offer," Denni said. "Thank you. But we can pay for supplies. You and your friends providing the manpower is more than generous."

Reece wasn't going to argue with her about it. But he had no intention of ever letting her see a bill for materials.

Only one question remained. How was he going to break the news to the guys?

Chapter Six

"Remind me why I'm up at seven in the morning on my first day off in two weeks." Joe's gravelly voice spoke of a guy who had just not-so-willingly crawled out of bed. He slammed the door of Reece's truck and belted himself in.

Reece tossed him a thermos of coffee, shifted into Drive and navigated the Avalanche away from the curb, heading toward Denni's street. "Because I've saved your carcass at least a hundred times. Besides I introduced you to Kelsey. You owe me."

Joe's sigh wasn't lost on Reece. "Kelsey's still sleeping."

Reece could pretty well figure why Joe didn't want to leave the warmth of his bed. At least the guy had a cute little pregnant wife to come home to at the end of the day.

"Can you two keep it down?" Sean, a rookie cop of six months, complained from the back seat. He'd been the only other sucker Reece could find to help out for the day. And if he'd had another few months of experience, Reece doubted he'd have been game. But lucky for Reece, the kid was still in that eager-to-please phase of his career.

Joe filled a disposable cup with the coffee and tossed the thermos back to Sean. "Here, this garbage Reece calls coffee is thick enough to wake you up and put hair on your chest."

Sean mumbled his thanks and turned back to Reece. "So what is it with this woman that you're giving up all your free time—and ours—to help her out? Is cracking this case really that important to you? Or is it the girl?"

Reece could feel his partner's eyes upon him, those scrutinizing baby blues that had forced a testimony from more than one reluctant witness in his seven years in the Rolla PD.

"Hey, maybe I'm just a nice guy."

Joe chortled. "Since when?"

A black figure darted out in front of the truck, breaking off all conversation.

Reece jumped on the brake and the Avalanche came to a screeching halt.

"What the…" Joe sputtered as hot coffee spilled down his front.

"Buffy!"

Reece recognized the name of the Doberman and slammed the gear shift into Park right in the middle of the street. He got out and strode toward the old lady. The woman trembled, her face red and her lips pushed out in indignation. "You almost killed my dog! Are you all right, my little sweet 'ums?" The dog had initially cowered in front of the truck as though realizing its mortality. But now, secure in the presence of her mistress,

Buffy bared her teeth and growled as Reece and the other two guys approached.

"Why is Buffy running around without a leash?" He fixed the woman with a stern, albeit respectful tone.

"I was just coming to get her with this." The old lady shook a pink leash at him.

"I thought I told you last time we met that she has to be restrained at all times."

The woman gaped. "Even when she's just going out to do her business?"

"Yes, ma'am. At all times."

"I put her out the back door and she keeps getting over her fence. I don't see what I'm supposed to do about that."

"That's for you to figure out, ma'am. It's against the law and punishable by a fine for Buffy to roam free."

She pulled herself to her full height, which couldn't have been more than four-nine. "I don't believe you're really a police officer. I've never seen you in a police car or uniform. What are you trying to pull?"

Reece rolled his eyes and showed her his badge…for the second time.

She sniffed. "Anyone can get one of those fake things. I saw it on *America's Most Wanted*."

Sean's low whistle prevented a reply as Leigh Sommers jogged toward them.

"Hey, Corrigan. Harassing the local elderly, now? Watch it, Mrs. James. The detective's a real crackerjack. Better not be hiding anything."

"You just watch yourself, missy, and don't worry about me," the woman shot back. "I can take care of myself."

As she passed, Leigh gave the old lady a salute. "You

got it. See you in a few, Corrigan. If you can find your way out of the middle of the street."

Reece scowled after her, then wheeled back around at the sound of Mrs. James's outraged voice.

"I'm calling the police and checking on your credentials. For all I know you're a drug dealer. Or a pimp!"

Joe and Sean let out simultaneous hoots of laughter.

"That's enough, guys," Reece muttered, before turning his attention back to the elderly woman. "Mrs. James, was it?"

"I'm not telling you a thing until I verify your identity."

With a sigh, he pulled a notepad from his pocket and jotted down his name and badge number. "Here, this should make it easier for you."

She harrumphed and tugged on the Doberman's leash. "Come along, Buffy."

The dog gave one more warning growl and followed her mistress.

A horn blared and Reece turned to find a line of four cars behind his truck. With a groan, he called out to the guys, "Go on up to the house." He pointed to Mahoney House. "I'll be there in a sec."

A minute later, he turned into the driveway and parked. He sat alone in the truck, staring at his partners seated on the step. This day wasn't starting off very well. Maybe he should just cut his losses and leave Denni Mahoney to her own devices. So he failed to crack one case in dozens. What would that matter in the grand scheme of things?

The door opened and Denni stepped out. She gave Sean and Joe a shy smile and offered her hand.

Who was he kidding? He was in this for the long haul. As long as Denni needed him—even if she didn't think she did—he'd be there to look out for her.

* * *

Denni took mental inventory of her looks. She was going for that understated look that says, "I have class, but I'm not a girlie-girl afraid of a little hard outdoorsy work."

Dressed in a comfortable pair of jeans, a light-blue pullover shirt with three buttons at the collar, and a pair of running shoes, she felt as though she'd accomplished her objective. A hint of mascara, powder and just a touch of lip gloss finished the look.

Fifty-percent humidity caused her hair to spring a bit at the temples, but Denni had never hated her curly hair the way her sister Keri hated hers. It was anyone's guess why the two of them had turned out with varying shades of red curls, while their older sister, Raven had hair as black as—well—a raven. And not even a hint of wave, let alone curls.

The sight of Reece striding up her lawn carrying a toolbox brought a smile to Denni's lips.

"Morning." He flashed her a smile.

She returned the infectious smile. "Thank you for coming. I hope you haven't had breakfast. I baked cinnamon rolls for you and your—um—crew."

His face reddened. "Three capable men are better than a dozen guys who don't know squat about what they're doing."

"So where's the other nine?" Leigh's voice shot over Denni's shoulder from behind. Denni moved aside and let the girl step out onto the porch. She smelled of floral soap and shampoo. Denni had never known her to shower and get downstairs so quickly after her morning run. Had she developed a sudden crush on Reece? Denni frowned.

The younger of Reece's companions chuckled. "I

think we've just been insulted." He shot Leigh an appreciative glance and a smile that Denni had a feeling was more than casual. No wonder Leigh had hurried. Relief flooded her. And she fought the urge to burst out laughing at the absurdity of her momentary suspicion.

Sean gave Leigh a lazy grin. She had definitely caught his attention. "You planning to stick around and give us a hand?"

"Ha! Me? I don't think I could bear to be in the same environment as all that blatant masculinity," she shot back, her pierced nose high in the air.

"I dare ya."

Denni smiled, then clenched her lips together as Leigh glared at her. Oh, this guy definitely had Leigh's number. Denni caught Reece staring at her. His brow was furrowed in a frown that clearly told her to call Leigh off.

Whether or not Leigh caught Reece's scowl and decided to do it just to bug him, or whether she did it because she honestly liked Sean—and who wouldn't?—Denni wasn't sure, but the next words from the girl were, "You're on. But I gotta warn you. I did Habitat for Humanity three years in a row. I can hold my own with a hammer."

She'd helped build homes for the poor? Denni had had no idea.

"Then let's get to work," Joe said, obviously adept at breaking tension where Reece was concerned. And Denni had a feeling that that was often.

"Hey, I thought the lady mentioned something about homemade cinnamon rolls." Sean's good-natured reminder spurred Denni to action.

"That's right. Never let it be said I sent a group of workers out on empty stomachs."

Reece grasped her elbow and pulled her back while the others made their way to the kitchen.

"Hey, that kid has the potential to be a great cop. I don't want Leigh ruining him."

Maternal indignation shot through Denni. "And Leigh has the potential to be a fantastic physical therapist. Maybe I don't want her getting distracted by some over-testosteroned cop-jock. What are you going to do about that?"

His brows shot up. "Over-testosteroned?" He nodded, his eyes crinkling in amusement. "I guess I'll have to give you that one. They can hold their own with each other."

"Then we're staying out of it?"

"I will, if you will."

"Deal. Wait until you taste one of my cinnamon rolls. You won't be thinking about anything else but how they melt in your mouth."

"I can't wait," he murmured, his tone suddenly husky. Just because she'd mentioned cinnamon rolls? Maybe the way to a man's heart really was through his stomach.

"It's the least I can do." Denni's voice sounded hoarse. "After all, you are getting me out of a major bind."

"Tell me about the old woman next door."

His capacity to shift gears so quickly left Denni a little off-guard. With a sister and a dad who were cops, she knew it was a professional tactic, but it was unsettling nonetheless. Still, after a few months of knowing Reece, she was beginning to go with the quick turns and not let the sudden changes of conversation throw her.

"Mrs. James? What about her?"

"She seems pretty determined that the girls are up to no good."

"You've been talking to my neighbors about the girls?"

Anger started to build. Just when she was beginning to ease into a comfortable camaraderie with him. "Why would you do that?"

"I'm investigating a crime. I've questioned *all* of your neighbors at one time or the other."

"I see. And as soon as you discovered Mrs. James was home you pounced on her?"

"Actually, her dog almost attacked me. But that's beside the point. Where has she been?"

"She's spent the last two winters in Florida with her daughter and son-in-law."

"Is there a Mr. James?"

"No. He passed on three years ago. I think that's the real reason Mrs. James leaves for all those months. She can't bear the loneliness. Her only other companionship is from a fifty-year-old daughter who is mentally ill."

"A daughter?"

Denni nodded. "Sarah. She doesn't venture out much and when she does, she doesn't speak. The loneliness is part of the reason Mrs. James got Buffy. That dog means everything to her."

"You got that right. I thought the old lady was going to take a stick to me for daring to defend myself against that monster." His chuckle brought a smile to Denni's lips.

"She really isn't so bad. She just can't believe that foster girls aren't necessarily juvenile delinquents."

"So she told me. In no uncertain terms."

"Well, she happens to be my next project, after I get my funding squared away."

He peered closer. "Mrs. James is a project?"

"She's so lonely. I know that's why she seems so mean."

"You think you can fix her?"

Ironic that he should use the word *fix*.

"People are so broken, Reece." Her voice choked. "I wish I could fix them all. But I can't."

He took her hand, almost as though trying to comfort her. Did he hear how her heart cried out for the hurting people of the world? People like Mrs. James. People like her girls, who had been rejected and in some cases abused? People like him…

"Then why do you try so hard?" he asked, his eyes piercing hers, searching for truth.

She covered their joined hands with her other one. "Because I know someone who can heal anyone. No matter how broken. He was broken first, so that I could be healed and whole. And not just me, but you, too. And Mrs. James and anyone who will call on His name."

For a second, Reece's face softened; his eyes seemed to accept what she was saying. Then, as quickly as the acceptance appeared, rejection followed, and hard lines appeared on his face. In one motion, they released each other.

"I'm not into religion, Denni. I know better."

"Oh, Reece. I'm not talking about religion. I'm talking about a man. Like you."

"Baby, don't flatter me. I'm no one's savior."

"I didn't mean you were a savior. I meant that He too was rejected by those He loved. He knows how you feel."

Reece sucked in a sharp breath. "What are you talking about?"

Denni stepped back in alarm. "I—I…nothing. Just…in the basement that night. When I asked you about family, you said 'which one.' I just assumed that you had grown up in foster care. Or at the very least that you'd been passed around among members of your own family."

"It's that obvious?" He seemed horrified by the thought of anyone knowing.

"Only to a social worker, probably."

"All right. So you know I don't have family and I was raised a ward of the state. That little tidbit of information goes no farther than this room. Understood? I can't have the girls thinking they can play on my emotional scars."

"They wouldn't..."

He fixed her with a hard look. "Understood?"

Hurt wound like a chain around her heart. Would he ever lower his guard? She nodded. "Understood."

Turning her back, she walked toward the kitchen, sensing his eyes upon her. The more she got to know him, the more she realized Reece Corrigan was a complex man, very capable of breaking her fragile heart. But that knowledge didn't stop her from offering it to him over and over on a silver platter. Would he ever see her as someone to cherish? And more importantly, would he ever give God another chance?

Chapter Seven

Reece watched, spellbound, as Denni stood before a congregation of at least five hundred people and spoke with great passion about her vision for Mahoney House.

Following a hunch, he'd attended the service in order to keep an eye on Elizabeth Wilson. As far as he was concerned, going to church went above and beyond the call of duty. He was definitely putting in for overtime on this one. But he needed to do some sniffing around without alerting Elizabeth to his instinct about her. Going to the service seemed to be the best way to get close.

After the luncheon, he'd done a little checking and found out she'd been turned down as a foster parent. That alone had raised his suspicion. In a state desperate for homes in which to place children, why would Missouri DFS turn down a woman who worked for a church? Then he'd discovered her little secret. Black-market prescription painkillers—supposedly for her cancer-riddled mother. Regardless of whether she had been telling the truth or not, she had been sentenced to rehab, probation and a mark on her permanent record.

He still didn't know what that had to do with Denni and knew he'd be laughed out of the department if he tried to make a case out of it. But Denni's position as a social worker, Elizabeth's sister scheduled to cater the luncheon which then got cancelled, Elizabeth getting turned down—all those things seemed to fit together, even if not quite perfectly. There were enough questions, as far as he was concerned, for him to take a closer look at the woman.

Denni's sweet voice lifted above his thoughts, causing him to refocus. "The state only guarantees children a home until they're eighteen," she said. "At that point, unless they've made a real familial connection with their foster family, they are on their own."

Her voice trembled, though from nerves or emotion, Reece couldn't be sure. Whichever the case, his heart went out to her. She was trying hard for these kids. Too hard, most likely. He glanced at the line of girls sitting shoulder to shoulder on the third pew six rows ahead of Reece. At least they listened to their benefactress with undivided attention—oops, he'd thought too soon— Leigh glanced at her watch at the same time that Fran hid a yawn behind her hand.

Irritation nagged him. He turned his attention back to Denni. She faltered a split second as their eyes locked. He gave her a reassuring smile and nodded.

"I—I believe this is something God has asked me to do, and I know that He will provide all of my needs. I've been amazed at his provision so far." Her lips curved into a smile and she sent Reece a pointed glance before turning back to the pastor. "Thank you for your time."

Reece fidgeted in his seat as he watched her hand the mike back to the minister and take her place next to

Leigh. That last look from her could have meant only one thing. She considered his offer to help with her home repair to be direct provision from the Almighty.

What a laugh. He was no one's answer to prayer. If God wanted to help Denni, He'd be more likely to send her a stable contractor with a heart of gold and a soft spot for orphans and the homeless. Not a cynical career cop with his own agenda.

Okay, sure. Maybe he did want to help Denni out of a bind. As a means to an end. But if there were nothing in it for him—a chance to find out more about the girls, the neighbor and now Elizabeth Wilson, for instance— Reece highly doubted his interest in Denni would be enough to warrant all the trouble.

As if sensing his attention, she turned and captured his gaze. Her smile quickened his pulse. Or was it only a means to an end after all? There was no denying the fact that he was attracted to Denni. Too attracted, most likely. He knew enough about religious women to know that even if she had any sort of feelings for him, her feelings for God were stronger and would prevent a relationship with anyone who didn't believe the same way.

Deep in thought, he startled to attention when the entire row stood. Dismissal music flooded the room. Denni leaned over and whispered something to Leigh. The girl scowled, her gaze darting to Reece.

Reece sent her a two-fingered salute. From the glare he received, he could only surmise that if she could've gotten away with it, the girl would have stuck out her tongue. He didn't bother to bite back his grin.

He remained still as Denni approached him, a delighted smile lighting her face. "Reece, it's wonderful to see you."

Drawn in by her warmth, Reece accepted the hand she offered and gave it a squeeze. "You gave a pretty compelling speech."

A blush flooded her cheeks. "Thanks. I hope it helps when the powers that be make their decision."

A throat being cleared behind them interrupted. "Excuse me. I need a moment of your time, Denni." Elizabeth Wilson's high-and-mighty tone acted like a wet blanket, dousing any flame of interest between Reece and Denni. For the moment, anyway. The woman gave him a high-browed once-over. "Detective...Corey, was it?"

"Corrigan," he replied, finding it difficult not to grit his teeth.

"Did you need something, Elizabeth?" Denni asked.

"I still haven't received your application for the grant. We can't really make a decision until you submit it, can we?"

"I didn't realize I had to submit another application since I *am* reapplying for the same grant. But if I do, I'll pick one up this week."

"New policy. I sent you one two weeks ago."

"I didn't get it."

"I'll send another one tomorrow. Please try not to misplace it. We're running out of time."

Denni's eyes narrowed and sparkled with anger, but to her credit, she held her tongue as the self-important woman said goodbye and walked away.

"She must have forgotten to send it," Denni muttered.

"Either that or someone conveniently forgot to give it to you."

"Don't start. Detective."

"Just doing my job."

"This is a day of rest. So *give* it a rest, will you?"

Unable to resist a grin, Reece nodded. "Okay, but only if you'll go to lunch with me."

"Actually, I came over to see if you want to have a late lunch—or early supper, if you prefer—at the house. We're trying out the new deck you and your crew so kindly fixed for us. The barbecue grill is all cleaned and ready for chicken, hamburgers and hot dogs. Sean already invited himself to join us, so you might as well come too."

"Sean invited himself to dinner?"

Amusement tipped one corner of her lips. "He's been over every day since your work day. Leigh pretends to be annoyed, but I think she's mostly afraid to let herself hope he's really interested."

"He doesn't seem the sort to play with a girl's feelings."

"They rarely do. But you never can tell when someone has an ulterior motive, can you?"

Unease crept through him. Was she fishing? Warning? He forced himself to keep eye contact when he really wanted to sink through the floor to hide from her knowing gaze.

"So, what time is this barbecue?"

After another second of scrutiny, she seemed to let it go. "Around three."

"Can I bring anything?"

"You've done enough for us. This is our treat."

On the verge of telling her she didn't owe him anything and that doing things for her was his pleasure, Reece stifled a growl when Leigh's voice shut him down.

"Coming, Denni?"

"Yeah." She touched Reece's arm with slender fingers. "See you later, then?"

"Yep. I'll be there."

Her eyes lit with pleasure as she turned to join her girls.

* * *

"He's here." Fran's flat tone could mean only one person. Denni turned away from the grilling burgers. She nearly dropped her spatula at the sight of Reece, dressed in khaki shorts and a black T-shirt. Leather loafers finished off a casual, Rhett Butler sort of nonchalance that never failed to make Denni sweat. Reece was just cool. And probably way out of her league.

"I told you not to bring anything." She nodded at the enormous watermelon cradled like a puppy in his arms.

"Sorry, it's in my nature to bring something to a barbecue. Didn't figure a six-pack would win me any points."

"It would have won you points with me," Fran quipped.

Denni scowled at him as if to say, Now see what you've started?

"Next time I'll bring one, then," Reece said, ruffling Fran's hair. "A six-pack of soda."

"Hey, watch the hair, Corrigan!" But her voice lifted with amusement. She aimed her sports water bottle at him and squeezed.

Reece sucked in a breath as the ice-cold water spotted the front of his shirt. "You little twerp!" He chuckled despite the confrontational words and snatched up a bottle of water from the large ice cooler next to the kitchen door.

With a squeal, Fran took off at a run.

Denni laughed, watching the scene unfold. Reece caught up with Fran without too much effort, capturing her in a headlock.

Fran screamed as he squeezed water over her head. Both were laughing when he let her go. Fran pointed her bottle at him again. Reece raised both hands. "Truce?"

"Sure, truce."

Denni could see by the glint in her eye that the girl had no intention of allowing a truce just yet. Not when Reece had gotten the last squirt. She was about to warn Reece when she noticed his arm shoot out at the same time Fran's did. Water streamed from both bottles. Denni shook her head. They deserved each other.

And the laughter started all over again.

Denni loved the sound of that laughter. When was the last time she'd seen Fran do anything playful? The girl had been under so much tension trying to find a job and keeping up with school that all she ever did was growl anymore. Maybe Reece's attention today would bring her back to her old self again. Prospects were looking up anyway.

The kitchen door slid open and Shelley stepped out just as the chicken reached the point where it was necessary to take it off the grill or serve it up as a burnt offering.

"Oh, Shelley, hand me that tray, will you?"

"Sure."

She lifted the platter from the patio table and held it out. Fran's laughter echoed through the air. Denni reached for the tray and caught a glimpse of Shelley's face darkening as she watched the playful antics.

"Is there a problem?" Denni asked.

Shelley blinked back to attention. "No. Just surprised, that's all. When did the queen of mean get so friendly with Kojak?"

Denni snickered at the reference to the bald-headed cop. "All he needs is a lollipop."

"So what gives with those two anyway? New romance or a father figure?"

Alarm shot through Denni. Surely not romance? Or

did Reece like younger women? "I don't know. Friends maybe? They both like to play." She glanced across the yard. Fran was on her way back to the deck. Reece seemed to be focused on Mrs. James's backyard.

"Yeah, who'd have thought it of either of them?"

A breathless and soaked Fran climbed the steps onto the deck, her face shining with pleasure. "I'll be back to help out in a sec, Denni. I have to change my shirt."

"New boyfriend?" Shelley baited.

"Gross." Fran threw her a look of disdain and disappeared through the sliding glass door into the house.

Denni's lips twitched, as relief flooded her. "Guess that answers that little question."

Shelley chuckled. "I guess. Kojak wouldn't appreciate the sentiment, though."

"Stop calling him that. He's going to hear you." She tossed a towel at the girl and laughed despite her admonishment.

Grinning, Shelley grabbed a stalk of broccoli from the enormous salad bowl. "You think he's never heard it before?"

"Maybe so, but it's a little insulting."

"Then maybe he ought to let his hair grow out." She frowned. "What's he doing, anyway?"

"What?"

"Corrigan. He's doing something to Mrs. James's fence."

Denni followed Shelley's gaze. Reece bent and studied something at the bottom of the fence, then stood up.

He turned, as though in thought, and noticed his audience. He waved and headed toward the deck just as Leigh and Sean joined the group from inside.

"Hi everyone," Sean said.

Denni smiled at their laced fingers. *Oh, Lord. Please protect Leigh's tender heart.*

She turned to Reece. "What's up with Mrs. James's yard?"

"Just trying to see how Buffy keeps getting through her fence." He shrugged. "I didn't see any weak spots in the fence, though."

"That's because she jumps it, genius." Leigh rolled her eyes.

Reece's eyebrows shot up. A giggle bubbled to Denni's lips. He had to admit the girl had one-upped him this time. His lips twisted into a sheepish grin. "Why didn't I think of that?"

Leigh shrugged, refusing to join in the camaraderie if it meant sharing a laugh with Reece.

"What do you think, Sean? Got another project in you?"

"What kind of project?"

"I'm thinking maybe we should add a foot or two to Mrs. James's fence."

"The battleax that called you a pimp?"

Leigh, Fran and Shelley let up a howl.

"She called you a pimp?" Fran asked, nearly out of breath. "I suppose we're your stable of fillies?"

"Presumably." Sean grinned at her. Leigh shifted beside him, her eyes narrowing. Jealousy?

"I think that would be really nice of you." Denni smiled at Reece. "And I'd feel a lot safer without Buffy roaming around growling at everyone."

"Me too." Reece's gaze captured hers and Denni read volumes of meaning in the two-word sentence.

He wanted to keep her safe, but there had to be another reason he played the hero.

Chapter Eight

Reece kicked back in a cushioned patio chair on Denni's deck. The chair had seen better days as far as he was concerned. He shifted as a rough seam in the material rubbed against his bare legs.

Sean sat next to him and they watched as the girls tossed a Frisbee in the yard.

Leigh turned toward them. "Hurry up you two."

"In a minute," Sean called back. "Let our food settle a little. We ate more than you."

"Wimp!" she shot back with a teasing grin.

Sean chuckled.

"So, that Leigh…" Reece began, then regretted ever mentioning her. Now what did he say to follow up? She's a real sweet girl? Not even close. Pretty? She could be without the piercings and black dye.

"I've seen her before," Sean said.

"Quite a lot, from what I hear. Denni said you've been a regular fixture around here since last week."

"Yeah. But I mean I recognized her from somewhere when we came last week." He shook his head and stared closer at the girl. "I can't put my finger on where, though. That's why I've been hanging around so much. I just have a hunch."

"You mean you're investigating? Not really interested in her?"

The rookie shrugged. "She's a lot more normal than I thought she would be at first. But taking her home to meet Mom and Dad? I doubt that. My mom's a member of the Daughters of the American Revolution."

Reece frowned. "Hey, she's got feelings. Just don't forget that."

"You're one to talk. I thought I'd just help you out. You're going after the housemother. I'm concentrating on the girl. Fran's sort of cute too. I might spend a little time with her if I can manage it without Leigh getting suspicious. Unless you have plans to work on Fran?"

"She's a kid."

"I saw your water fight earlier."

Incredulity sprang inside of him. "We were just kidding around. Like I said, she's just a kid."

"Okay, then. I'll take the younger girls, as I can get by with it, and you concentrate on Miss Mahoney."

Surprise sucked the words out of Reece's brain. He stared at Sean. "You think I'm playing with Denni's emotions to help the investigation?"

"Well, let's see… You haven't had a date with the same woman twice since I've known you."

"That you know of."

"Have you?"

"Well, no."

"Okay. It's obvious this wholesome woman isn't your type, but you seem to go out of your way to spend time with her. So I figured out that you're playing her to get closer to the investigation."

It sounded pretty low-down when verbalized by someone who obviously didn't have a problem with doing whatever it took to bring in the guilty party. "I like Denni," he said, noting how insincere his voice sounded.

"Oh, sure. I like Leigh too. I'm not saying this case isn't going to have its rewards." He laughed as only a twenty-year-old guy can. "I'm just saying that two heads are better than one. A couple of good-looking guys like us, hanging around a bunch of women, we'll get this case wrapped up in no time."

"Hey, heads up!" Leigh called.

The Frisbee sailed through the air toward them. Sean hopped up and caught it effortlessly. "All right. I'm coming." He glanced down at Reece. "You going to play?"

"I don't think so. Denni's headed this way."

Sean gave him a knowing grin before jumping over the deck rail and joining the game.

Denni climbed the steps to the deck. She smiled at Reece. "I'm definitely not in shape. I'm worn out. Amazing how I forget I'm not still eighteen until I hang out with a couple of eighteen-year-olds."

Reece chuckled. "I know what you mean."

She rolled her eyes. "Sure you do."

"You don't believe me?"

"I'd say you're in pretty good shape. You could probably run circles around them."

"So you've noticed my buffed physique, huh?"

Reece enjoyed the quick rise of color to her cheeks. "Do you want to go for a walk?"

"Sure," she replied. "Let me go inside and grab my tennies."

"Tennies?"

"Walking shoes. We called them tennies when I was a kid. I guess I'm not grown up yet."

"I think it's cute."

The flush returned. "Thanks. I'll be right back."

Reece watched her enter the house. What had Sean meant about Denni obviously not being his type? What sort of woman did the rookie think he was looking for? A rough, beer-drinking, cussing biker chick? He might have wanted that when he was younger. A woman to have fun with without any kind of commitment. And he wasn't even hinting to himself that he wanted a relationship. But lately, he couldn't get interested in anyone. His usual casual dates held no appeal.

When was the last time he'd even stepped inside the local sports bar to wind down at the end of a shift? A long time. Months. Was he getting soft or just old?

The best times he'd had lately were the luncheon, the work day, today... Being with Denni. Hmmm. Was she getting under his skin? He certainly wasn't any closer to figuring out who was trying to shut her down than he had been two weeks ago. Or two months ago for that matter.

The door slid open and he looked up, his heart lurching at the sight of her bathed in the bright light of the late-afternoon sun.

One thing was for certain. His feelings were definitely entering the arena. This couldn't be good. Not for him. Not for Denni. How was he going to be objective now that his palms were itching to hold her hand? Now that he knew that he was feeling something for her that went beyond a desire to see justice prevail on her behalf? He wanted more than that. He wanted to see her safe, happy, her dreams and goals fulfilled.

Love had eluded him for his entire adult life. Were his feelings betraying him after he had carefully avoided entanglements all these years?

"Ready to go?" Denni smiled. She had changed into a pair of gray shorts and a light-pink tank top. He stared at the soft curves of her calves and shoulders.

"What?" she asked, seeming a bit flustered by his attention.

"Nothing. Let's go." He reached out and snatched her hand.

She glanced up at him, alarm in her eyes. But before he could apologize and let it go, she curled her fingers through his. Reece swallowed hard. Her small, soft hand inside his evoked strange new sensations inside his chest.

"Hey, where are you two going?"

Shelley's voice snapped him back to the moment.

"For a walk," Denni replied.

"Don't forget curfew." Fran's voice rang with amusement.

A smile tipped Denni's lips. "Don't worry. I won't."

"You two have fun," Sean called. He gave Reece a thumbs-up.

"What's that all about?" Denni asked.

Reece tightened his fingers around hers and gave her a sideways grin. "You know how guys are."

"Not really," she muttered.

Guilt splayed through his chest. He had the uncomfortable feeling he was taking advantage. Denni obviously hadn't had much experience with men. Would he be able to get what he needed from the relationship and still salvage the good parts at the end of the day? He knew his feelings for her were real. When all this was over, he'd have to find a way to convince her. Hopefully it wouldn't be too late.

Still the case had to be solved. He didn't have that much time to do it. The chief had made it pretty clear: either solve it soon or file it away.

So far, Denni had been stolen from, her basement sabotaged. Next time the harm could be to her personally. The thought made him tighten his fingers. She looked up at him, questions written in her eyes.

He loosened his grip, but determination pressed him. He wouldn't let Denni be hurt. Even if it meant he risked losing her when it was all over.

Denni leaned back against her pillow, a book resting on her bent knees. Not that she could concentrate on one word. The memory of Reece's long fingers laced with hers permeated every thought, causing butterflies to flutter in her stomach. The romance novel she was attempting to read couldn't compete with the reality of their walk. Of the entire day, really.

A slow smile lifted the corners of her lips. They'd enjoyed a few moments alone. Shoulder to shoulder, hand in hand. What was it about this guy that made her heart race?

Dad had been a cop before retiring. Was that it? The whole adage about a girl marrying a man just like her dad?

She laughed at her foolishness, then sobered as a thought made its way into her mind.

True, Reece was like her dad, Mac Mahoney, in lot of ways. Strong, a servant of the people, stubborn to be sure. But in the way that mattered most, they were nothing alike. Mac loved God above all else. Reece admitted he had no use for religion.

Her dreams crashed as this reality drove home. She had been so caught up in the surprise of his grabbing her hand, that she hadn't even considered the impossibility of a romantic relationship between them.

Her cell phone chirped Beethoven's Für Elise—Raven's ring. She glanced at the clock next to her bed. Figured, only Raven would call her at eleven at night. Just as well, she was about to start getting really depressed over the whole Reece issue. She snatched up her phone from the nightstand.

"Hey, Rave. What's up?"

"Can't I call my sister even if nothing's up?"

Denni laid the romance novel face down on her end table and sank under her comforter. "You could, but you don't."

"Well, how honest of you to say so." Raven sounded amused and maybe a bit offended.

"Everything okay?"

"Yeah. I guess."

Denni rolled her eyes at the ritual and glanced at the clock again—11:02. It would be at least 11:05 before she could pull the truth out of Raven. Usually, work was the reason for her melancholy. "So how are things going at the station?"

"All right, I guess. I found out tonight that Tom's getting ready to retire."

Bingo. That didn't take long.

"Really? You going after the anchor slot?"

"Duh. That's been my goal for the last ten years. I thought the guy would never give it up. I mean he has to be at least seventy-five."

"So why is this a problem?"

"I thought I said there was no problem?"

"Okay, fine. Everything is just hunky-dorey." Denni turned her hand over and winced at her chipped nails. She reached to her right and fumbled in the nightstand drawer for a file.

"Man. What has you in a bad mood tonight?"

"Nothing."

"All right. Listen. You tell me what's wrong with you and I'll tell you what's wrong with me. Okay?"

It was a game they'd played since they were kids. "Fine. You go first."

"All right. The station manager's daughter also has her eye on the anchor position."

"Becca? But she just got out of college. Surely they won't give it to her."

"Nepotism is a powerful force. And the force is unusually strong with Becca."

Denni snickered at Raven's impression of Darth Vader. "I just can't believe they'd do something so blatantly unfair."

"Well, believe it."

"All right. Let's think. You need to come up with a spectacular story. One that will blow the socks off those guys in charge."

"Spectacular stories are in short supply, unfortunately."

"You could always do something about a social worker who…oh I don't know, say is trying to open a couple of houses for former foster-care girls…that might drum up some interest."

"For you, but probably not for me."

"All right." Denni tried to swallow the hurt and remember that her sister was the only Mahoney who currently wasn't serving God.

"Hey, Denni. I'll run the idea by Charles and see if he'll okay it."

Denni hesitated. "I don't want to force you into anything."

"Are you kidding? A bleeding-heart story will make me look really good. Just think about what all that positive mail will do for my chances of getting the anchor position."

Denni laughed. "Well, I'm glad my bleeding heart is good for something."

"Okay, your turn."

Denni had pretty much talked herself out of spilling it about Reece. Besides, Raven wasn't going to agree with her commitment not to get involved with an unbeliever. The "unequally yoked" rule didn't impress her. Nor did anything else about the Christian life. She didn't speak her disapproval aloud, but Denni knew she felt just a little superior…a little more enlightened than the rest of the family.

"Come on, Denni. A deal's a deal."

"Okay. There's this guy…"

"Oh?" Raven's voice lifted with interest and teasing.

"Yeah, but don't get too excited. He's the cop investigating the break-in from a couple months ago."

"Corrigan?"

"Good memory. Yeah. Reece."

"So you're dating him?"

"No. Nothing like that." Denni paused, wishing she'd never brought it up.

"What then?"

Realizing her inquisitive reporter of a sister wasn't going to give it a rest until she got the story, Denni told it all. From the break-in and Reece's suspicions, to the water in the basement and Reece coming to her rescue, and finally to the wonderful warmth of his large hands wrapping around hers this evening.

"So what's the problem? Sounds like he really likes you."

"Did you hear anything besides the part where he held my hand?" Denni chuckled.

"I'm not saying there won't be kinks to work out. But when was the last time you were interested in a guy?"

"You mean, when was the last time someone was actually interested in me, don't you?"

"Either way. Don't throw it away just because he's the one looking into the stuff going on around there. Sounds to me like he might actually have a point with the girls."

"Not really. Why would they want to take a chance on getting kicked out of their home if I had to close it down?"

"Who knows? But even if he's wrong about that, don't give up without exploring the possibilities. There aren't enough guys left in the world who can make a girl's heart go pitter-patter."

"Well, we'll see." As far as Denni could tell, there was no point in bringing up the main reason a relationship wasn't possible. Raven would just turn it around and be defensive. And eleven-thirty at night was too late to get into that kind of argument. Besides, it smelled like something was…burning.

Denni pushed back the covers and padded to her door. She gasped as a haze confronted her.

"Rave, I have to go. I think there might be a fire."

She pushed the button to disconnect the call before Raven could say anything else.

"Girls, get up," Denni hollered. Flying down the hall, she banged on each door. "There's a fire. Get up!"

By the time she banged on Shelley's and Cate's door, Fran and Rissa had stumbled from their shared room.

Cate ran out. "Shelley's not in the room!"

"Shelley!" Denni turned to Rissa. "Get Shelley, and get out of the house. I have to go down there."

She didn't see any glowing lights as she descended the stairs, so she could only hope the fire was small. Smoke burned her throat. She clasped her hand over her mouth and kept going toward the source of the smoke. She reached the kitchen with Leigh and Fran on her heels. Flames shot up from the stove, and inched toward the counter on either side of the stove top. Denni snatched the throw rug from the floor and beat at the flames.

For what seemed like an eternity she brought the rag rug up and back down over and over. She continued to struggle, only vaguely aware that Fran and Leigh had joined her in fighting the fire. She wanted to tell them to leave. Get out. Be safe, but she didn't have the energy to focus on anything but putting out the fire before it completely destroyed her home.

And the only words she could form sent a hoarse cry heavenward.

Chapter Nine

A fire truck and two cop cars were arrayed on the street in front of Denni's Victorian-style home by the time Reece whipped his Avalanche onto Clark Street. A quick message from Sean had alerted him to a 911 call the rookie had heard over the radio.

Reece parked half a block away and jogged to the house. He spotted Sean standing next to Leigh, his arms circling the slender girl. Sean dropped a tender kiss on Leigh's head and she snuggled close to him. To Reece, they looked like a couple in love. The kid was either a very good actor, or he cared more about Leigh than he wanted to admit.

Scanning the yard, Reece's gaze slid past firefighters, police officers, and the girls.

Where was Denni?

Finally, he spotted her alone, sitting on the steps. His heart did a skip, and tenderness welled up inside of him. He strode across the lawn.

She raised her chin and caught his gaze. Wordlessly,

Reece dropped down next to her and slipped his arm around her shoulders, pulling her close.

A shaky breath left her. "Thanks for coming over, Reece. You heard about the fire over the radio?"

"Sean called me."

She nodded.

"Do they know what happened yet?"

"The fire started on the stove."

"How?"

"Cate made some herbal tea and must have forgotten to turn off the burner under the pot."

"Cate?"

She gave a weary nod. "But don't read anything into it. She thought she'd turned it off. Cate's pretty conscientious. I can't imagine her being so forgetful."

"Then you think someone else did it on purpose and made it look like an accident?"

She snapped her head toward him and frowned. "I didn't say that."

"I think that's what you're implying." Reece kept his tone deliberately calm. Non-confrontational. "Can you tell me what's on your mind?"

"Everyone was upstairs except for Shelley." Her voice lagged and she expelled a heavy sigh.

"Where was she?"

She shrugged. "I don't know. She isn't home yet."

Reece glanced at his watch. "So much for curfew."

"Yeah."

"Do you think it could have been her?"

Again her eyes narrowed. "I told you, Shelley's not home. It couldn't have been her. And the rest of the girls were upstairs. I know they were because I hadn't been in bed long and I had just checked on them before I went into my room."

"Shelley was there when you went to bed, but now she's gone?" Didn't Denni understand how that looked to the average observer? If Shelley had set the fire, she wasn't too smart about covering her tracks.

"She wasn't in her room, but the bathroom light was on when I went by. I just assumed she was in there."

"Well, we're not going to know anything until she gets home. How much damage is there?"

"Just the stove and counters and a little bit of the wall behind the stove." She dropped her forehead into her palms. "When will all of this end? It's been just one disaster after another."

Her despair shot through his heart like an arrow.

"We'll get to the bottom of it, Denni." He squeezed her shoulder. "I promise."

"What if I'm just trying to orchestrate a greater purpose in life than God intends?"

"That's not exactly my area."

"Yeah," she gave another sigh. "I know it isn't, Reece."

She said the words with such sadness that Reece almost wished he had the kind of faith necessary to speak comforting words. At one time, he'd begun to develop a fragile faith in God. But that faith had been effectively quashed the day he'd stood over the dead bodies of people who had believed, like Denni, that they could make a difference. Some difference.

His gaze scanned the area. A fireman stood by the fence separating Mrs. James's yard from Denni's. The old lady clutched her housecoat tightly at her throat. She waved her hand toward Denni in what appeared to be an animated sort of accusation. Reece tensed.

"I'll be back," he said to Denni.

The firefighter seemed to be wrapping up his questioning when Reece reached the fence. Reece flashed his badge.

"Don't trust him," Mrs. James said to the firefighter. "He's Miss Mahoney's boyfriend."

Reece's ears warmed. "Actually, that isn't true."

"Then why are you always over there?"

"Because I'm helping Miss Mahoney fix some things around the house. As a friend." Not that it was any of her business.

She gave him a look that clearly conveyed her doubt.

Reece chose to ignore the dubious lift of her brow and tried to smile. "I am interested in what you have to add to this incident, Mrs. James."

"I don't have to tell you a thing." She sniffed.

Reece turned to the firefighter. "Are you satisfied that this was an accident?"

The man shrugged. "We'll have to wait and see what the investigation turns up. They were lucky Mrs. James was awake and noticed the smoke. She's the one who called us."

Reece's brow rose at the information. He turned to Mrs. James. "You always stay up that late?"

"Buffy needed to tinkle," she said with a dignified lift of her chin.

Or maybe you were sneaking back to your house and wanted to throw suspicion off yourself. But he kept the thought to himself.

"Well, I'm sure Miss Mahoney and her girls are grateful."

"I couldn't let them burn alive just because I don't approve of their lifestyle." She dismissed Reece and turned back to the fireman. "Is there anything else you need to ask me, sir?"

Her switch in tone from disdain to respect wasn't lost on Reece. He scowled.

"There's nothing more for now, ma'am," the firefighter replied. "But the investigators may want to question you further in the days ahead."

"Whatever I can do. As I said, I may not approve, but I wouldn't want them to die a horrible death in a fire."

"Yes, ma'am." The firefighter gave Reece a lopsided, she's-all-yours grin and moved away.

"If you ask me," Mrs. James said, and then continued even though he hadn't asked, "I think one of those girls did it."

"What makes you say that?"

"Buffy barked and barked. I couldn't make her stop. And that's just not like my baby. She's usually very obedient."

Sure she was. Reece eyed the elderly lady. "Maybe she saw a rabbit. Or squirrel."

"I saw a shadow run away from that house, and if it was a rabbit it was a mighty giant one."

Reece started and peered closer. Now this was some information he could work with. "Are you sure it was a human shadow?"

"I think I know what I saw and my daughter Sarah saw it too."

"All right. Which way did this person run?"

"I already told that other man. The shadow took off down the block." She pointed. "That way."

"Thank you, Mrs. James," Reece said. "I'll check it out."

"Is that all you want from me for tonight? I need my rest. And Sarah's getting nervous. I can tell."

"I'm sure anything else can wait until morning."

She gave a nod and a sniff and turned her back.

Watching her go, Reece shook his head. That lady really didn't like him. And she wasn't kidding. He grinned in spite of himself.

The fire truck and police cars pulled away, leaving Denni to pick up the pieces of the most recent disaster. He saw her still sitting on the steps, now surrounded by the girls. Sean stood away from them, as though he didn't want to impose.

Reece joined him.

Sean nodded toward the house. "So, I guess we'll be scheduling another work day at Mahoney House."

Reece grinned. "Is this something we can do, or will we have to get a professional?"

He shrugged. "I haven't seen it yet. The fire didn't make it out of the kitchen, though, so that's good news. I guess she has insurance."

"I'm sure."

"Think we ought to leave them alone? Or do we need to play the big strong heroes and stick around to offer our shoulders in case they want to cry?"

Sean's arrogance hit a raw nerve.

"I think if you aren't genuinely concerned about the fact that Leigh could have been hurt or even killed, then maybe you need to go ahead and leave." Reece scowled. "This is no time for your games."

"Hey, I didn't say I don't care." His gaze scanned the porch then rested on Leigh. "She's pretty tough on the outside, but she isn't always like that, you know."

"Can't say I'd noticed that." As far as Reece had

seen, the girl was tough as nails inside and out. Her wit was razor-sharp and he wasn't thrilled about being on the slicing end of her sarcastic remarks.

Denni rose and Reece went to her. "Will you be all right in the house or do you need to stay somewhere until it's all cleaned up?"

"We're fine. We'll have to deal with the smell of smoke, but there's no good reason not to stay here."

Reece admired her strength. "I'll be over sometime tomorrow to look around."

"Look around?"

"We won't know if it's an accident or arson for a few days, but I'd like to check on some things."

He braced himself for an argument as she met his gaze evenly. Instead of raising a fight, she nodded. "All right. Come over when it's convenient. I'll be here all day."

She released a heavy sigh. "Good night, Reece. Thank you for coming."

Feeling sufficiently dismissed, Reece turned and headed down the block toward his truck. He climbed in and slid the key into the ignition, but hesitated. The defeat on Denni's face played across his mind.

He wanted to pray. To ask God to help him find out who was sabotaging Denni's dream. But something held him back. He couldn't seem to grip the concept of giving over control of his life to someone else. As far as he was concerned, the very act of prayer insinuated that a person wasn't capable of making decisions without second-guessing oneself.

Reece cranked the engine and slowly pulled away from the curb.

No. God wasn't going to be the one to catch whoever

was doing these things to Denni. He'd had plenty of time if He was going to.

Reece figured he was pretty much on his own. He had every intention of cracking this case. And he was going to do it before one more act of sabotage, theft or much worse could occur.

He came to the stop sign at the end of the street, was just about to turn, when he noticed a pedestrian on the sidewalk. His heart gave a jerk. Had the arsonist come back? He took a closer look under the glow of the streetlight. The tall figure had the telltale feminine form. Slumped shoulders reminded him of… Shelley?

He whipped the Avalanche into reverse and backed up, then parked along the curb, waiting for her to approach. He rolled down the window. "Shelley?"

She jumped then pressed her palm against her chest. "Reece. You scared me to death. What are you doing around here so late?"

"Checking on Denni. I wanted to make sure she was okay after the fire." Smooth. He watched her expression closely.

Her brow lifted. "Fire? At our house? Is everyone okay?"

"Yeah. It started in the kitchen, on the stove apparently. Someone left a burner on."

"Cate! I've reminded her over and over about that teapot of hers."

"Oh, what makes you think it was Cate?"

She shrugged. "Who else? No one messes around the kitchen late at night except for Cate when the baby's kicking and she can't sleep. She always makes a cup of tea and works on her schoolwork in bed."

"I see." He opened the door and slid out. "Well, let me walk you back to the house."

"Okay. But it's only a half a block."

"Well, I'm a gentleman."

Shelley gave a snort. "There's a new word for you. We'll have to add that to the list."

"List?"

"Oh, sure. At the risk of giving away the family secrets. You've been called everything from Kojak to hottie."

In spite of himself, Reece felt his face warm. Girls talked about guys that way?

"Hottie I can live with. But Kojak?" He rubbed his head. "Bald is in."

"I know. We're just joking around to razz Denni, mostly."

"Denni?" He grinned and nudged her with his elbow. "Is there something you'd like to tell me?"

"No way! I've said too much already. You're on your own with Denni."

Reece gave a chuckle as they climbed the steps. Shelley moved her purse around from where it hung on her shoulder. She fumbled through the bag. Frowned. Shook the purse, then knelt on the porch and started removing items.

"Lose your key?"

"Yeah. You don't have to stick around," she said distractedly. "I'll find it."

"I'll wait until you get inside before I go back to the truck."

"My hero," she said with an exaggerated sigh.

After a futile search, she stood with a frustrated huff and patted her pockets. "I must have left it somewhere. I know I had it when I left earlier."

"Guess there's no sneaking in after curfew tonight."

"No kidding. Denni has enough to deal with after the fire. She doesn't need the added pressure of chewing me out."

Reece reached forward and pressed the doorbell. "Might as well get it over with."

Chapter Ten

Denni stared at the duo on her doorstep. Never in a million years would she have guessed that she'd answer the bell to find Shelley and Reece waiting. "What's going on?"

"I can't find my key," Shelley said, swinging her purse over her shoulder. "I'm sorry I'm late. The study session went on longer than I thought it would."

Denni inwardly gave her forehead a smack.

Now she remembered Shelley had told her about the study session. "Okay, that explains where you've been. Why is Reece bringing you home?" She lifted her gaze to his. "Were you at her study session, too?"

"Hardly." His lips twisted into a wry grin. "I saw her walking home and thought I'd tag along as protector."

Alarm shot through Denni. She focused her attention once more on Shelley. "Why were you walking home? You should have called me to come and get you."

"Mark offered to bring me, but I found out pretty quick that he's not the gentleman our detective, here, is."

Reece grinned and shrugged at Denni's questioning glance.

"Anyway, Mark got handsy and I made him pull over and let me out. The big jerk actually dropped me off a good mile and a half from here. I still wouldn't have made curfew, though. We lost track of time."

"Well, we won't talk about curfew, this time, since you were studying." She sent the girl an affectionate smile. "You've never given me reason to worry before. Did Reece tell you what happened?"

She nodded. "How bad is it?"

"The kitchen looks like we had a fire. And you can smell smoke all over the house, but I think we can get the clean-up done in a reasonable amount of time." She gave a long sigh. "The stove's ruined. And the counters will have to be redone."

Shelley scowled. "That's all we need right now. How are we going to do all that?"

Denni patted her arm. "Let's not worry about it for now. We'll think about that tomorrow."

"After all, tomorrow is another day," Shelley returned.

"Okay, Miss Scarlett, better get to bed. I'm going to need all the help I can get tomorrow cleaning up that kitchen."

Shelley gave her a quick hug. "I'm going to check out the damage, then go up to bed." She turned to Reece. "Thanks for being my knight in shining armor."

"No thanks necessary." His mouth drew up into a teasing smile. "That's just the kind of guy I am."

After Shelley left the room, Denni gathered a deep breath. It seemed she couldn't turn around without Reece being there lately.

"Are you doing all right?" Reece's voice seemed genuinely filled with concern. She wanted to believe it, but something niggled inside, raising her suspicions.

"I'm just glad no one was hurt or killed. The fire could have been so much worse."

"Have you given any more thought to who might have started it?"

A weary sigh escaped Denni's throat. "I think the fire investigator will conclude that it was an accident, started by the teapot on the stove."

Reece narrowed his eyes, but nodded. Denni's ire rose at the obvious patronizing.

"I mean it, Reece. There was no malice here, so just get that out of your head."

A wry grin split his lips. "My Kojak-bald head?"

Denni's jaw dropped. "Wh-what do you mean by that?"

"I know you and your girls are calling me Kojak behind my back."

"I never once…"

"Oh, it's okay. I'm just kidding." He rubbed his head. "Anyway, I guess I should be going so you can turn in."

"Reece?"

"Yeah."

"Do you want to come inside and have some hot chocolate with me?"

Surprise showed in his face and the lift of his eyebrows. "Are you sure? You have a pretty full day tomorrow."

"I'm wired. And…I guess I'd rather not be alone after all."

He took a step forward. "All right. I'd love to stay for awhile and keep you company."

She was keenly aware of his presence behind her as he followed her to the kitchen. She stopped short before entering.

"You okay?" he asked, close enough that she felt his breath against her hair.

"I forgot," she whispered. "I can't use the stove to boil the water." Her words caught in her throat.

"It's okay, honey." He moved around so that they faced each other in the doorway. He towered over her. Her face was inches from his neck, and she watched his Adam's apple bob as he swallowed hard.

Slowly, she lifted her chin to meet his gaze. Her mind clouded as he stared into her eyes. And she couldn't move. Had no desire to move. If only he would...

He searched her face and Denni didn't care if he saw her neediness at the moment. She did crave the comfort of his embrace. Keeping her eyes locked on his, she took a step forward.

He gathered a ragged breath. His arms crept around her and pulled her close. She drank in the spicy scent of aftershave and drew from his strength as she rested her head against his chest. With her arms tucked close to her body, she wouldn't exactly call this a hug. His heart beat a steady rhythm against her ear. For the first time all evening, she felt herself relax. She closed her eyes and drowsed against him.

"Denni," he whispered after what seemed like several minutes.

"Mmm?"

"I need to let you go."

Heat crept into her cheeks and she pulled back to look at him. "I'm sorry."

Despite his admission, he didn't release her. And she

didn't protest. "Don't be sorry. I enjoyed it," he said, pressing his forehead to hers. His voice dropped to a husky tone that tripped her stomach. "Probably more than I should, considering…"

Disappointment shot through Denni, and her muscles tensed again. "Considering you're determined to crack a nonexistent case?" She started to step out of his arms, but he tightened his hold and pulled her back.

"Considering everyone in the house has gone to bed and we're alone down here at 2:00 a.m."

"Oh," she mouthed.

His tone dipped along with his head. "Not to mention that for months I've wanted to do this…"

Warm lips covered hers before Denni could react. As her heart rate kicked into high gear, two parts of her brain played tug of war in her overloaded mind: the part that knew that this was impossible, given the difference in the way they lived their lives, and the part that wanted to press against Reece, slip her arms around his waist and surrender to his melting kiss. She didn't have to choose, as the kiss ended oh-so-soon.

"Reece," she whispered.

"Yeah, I know," he whispered back. He pressed a kiss to her forehead and slowly released his hold, never taking his eyes from hers. Recovering, he gave her a twisted grin. "If you feel the need to slap me, I'll stand strong and take it like a man."

With a short laugh, she stepped into the kitchen. "I think we'll just chalk this up to you trying to console me. I can let it go. Just…"

He held up his hand. "I know. Just don't let it happen again."

"Right. And I promise I'll be a rock when you're

around so you don't feel the need to offer me any more manly comfort."

She felt around for the flashlight on the counter and switched it on.

Reece whistled under his breath. "That fire did a number on your counter and wall. This isn't going to be cheap."

A groan escaped her in spite of her resolve to hold up whenever Reece was around. "I suppose I'll call the insurance agent in the morning. This is going to shoot my rates sky-high, but I don't have a choice, I'm afraid. A new stove, counter and the wall behind are going to cost a bundle. And don't offer to help, because I know this is way above your handyman skills."

She smiled to take the sting out of the words.

He studied the damage, rubbed a hand over his head and nodded. "Okay, you're right. I'd be as lost as a cow in a blizzard."

"I'm proud of you for admitting it."

He tossed her a lopsided grin. "It wasn't easy for a man with my level of pride."

"Well, you'll be a better man for it."

He gave her a brow-raised grin. "Don't be too sure."

She started to return his grin, then spied an object on the floor. Realizing what it was, she bent over and snatched it up.

"What's that?" Reece asked.

Facing him she tried to mold her face into the image of innocence. "Nothing."

He scowled. "What do you mean, nothing? I just saw you pick something up off the floor."

"Well, sheesh. Okay, if you're going to make a federal case out of it." She winced at her choice of words as she opened her fist and let him see.

He stared at her hand, confusion causing his brow to furrow. Then understanding dawned upon his expression and he nodded. "Shelley's key."

"Yeah," she said, hearing the dull tone of her voice. "Please don't read anything into this."

"Her key was in the kitchen, she wasn't here when the fire started, and she walked home. Denni…"

"No! Shelley loves me." Denni's lips trembled. "I know she wouldn't do anything to hurt me." She slapped her hand down hard on the counter. "I mean it, Reece. Please trust me. This is a coincidence."

Rolling his eyes, he frowned and shook his head. "No way. Give me the key. I want it for evidence."

"No. You can't have it."

"Listen to me." His voice was gruff. Gone was the tender man who had held her only a few moments earlier.

She squared her shoulders and braced herself. "Go ahead."

"You might think no one would possibly be out to hurt you, but someone obviously is. You even admitted after the flooded basement that someone is out to cause damage to this place. First there was the theft. Then there was the fire in the laundry room. Then the flooded basement and now this. The incidents are getting closer together which means that whoever did these things is getting impatient. You're going to have to let me do my job before something happens to you."

Denni's stomach turned over, not only at Reece's ominous prediction, but at his obvious concern—concern that went beyond his public servant role. "I know something isn't right. It's just so hard even to consider one of the girls capable of this. It must be someone else."

"So you're admitting these aren't random accidental mishaps?"

"I'm not stupid, Reece." Frustration loosened her tongue. "I told you before it might be sabotage. But for the life of me, I can't imagine why anyone would have a motive. If it's one of the girls, they'll be out of a home. If not…who?"

Reece shrugged. "Mrs. James doesn't seem too happy about the girls living here."

Waving away his suggestion, Denni shook her head. "No way. The lady's a little eccentric, and not mad about my girls, but she isn't a saboteur."

"How do you know?"

"Well, I just do." She peered closer to see if he was joking. "Reece. You can't possibly believe a sweet little old lady is capable of causing flooded basements and starting fires."

"I never rule anyone out based on age. And unless we're talking about two separate people, that Mrs. James isn't exactly *sweet*."

"Well, no. Probably not. But remember, the first incident wasn't sabotage, it was theft. And I can't exactly picture her breaking into the house and stealing."

"We never found evidence that anyone broke in," he reminded her. "I still think that was an inside job. And possibly unrelated to the three incidents of damage."

"You make my head ache with all of your theories." Denni leaned across the counter, pressing her palm against her forehead. "Find some proof to substantiate any of these so-called hunches, will you? I don't know how much more I can take."

"Believe me, I'm doing my best. It's only a matter of time, now. What about Sarah?"

"Sarah James?"

He nodded. "It's possible. Especially if she's nuts. That would explain the irrational incidents."

"She's not 'nuts' and you need some etiquette lessons."

"Funny, I'm not too concerned with etiquette when your safety is at stake."

Denni looked up at the hard tone. The stubborn set of his jaw left no doubt in her mind that he would beef up his investigation. Somehow, she couldn't quite decide if she should be relieved or worried.

Chapter Eleven

"You're going to have to wrap this up soon, Reece. We've already spent way too much time on a burglary case."

"It's more than burglary, Chief." Sitting across from his superior made Reece nervous. It wasn't often he was summoned to this office for something other than a pat on the back.

This time, however, was far different. And Denni's safety might very well depend upon Reece's ability to convince the chief that this case went beyond the obvious.

He could throttle Denni for failing to report the laundry-room fire and the flooding of her basement. He had the feeling that if Mrs. James hadn't called 911, the kitchen fire would have been dealt with using the sink sprayer and anything Denni could find to beat the flames.

But the file on the chief's desk didn't contain most of the incidents. Only the theft and the 911 call. The chief gave him a convince-me look.

"Look," Reece said, taking the friendship approach.

"You know me. I'm not going to waste the taxpayer's money on a frivolous case. First of all, we haven't recovered any of the items that were stolen."

"How close are you?"

Rubbing his hand over his head, Reece blew out a breath.

The chief nodded. "That's what I figured."

"Since that robbery, there have been three sabotage attempts. Someone doesn't want Mahoney House to stay open."

The chief glanced down at the skinny folder and back up to Reece. "I see that there was a fire a few nights ago, but it looks like an accident. There's nothing in this report about other incidents."

Reece scowled. "I know. Denni didn't report them."

"There you have it, then. Not much we can do about something that isn't reported." The chief's Groucho Marx brows pushed together and he leaned forward. "Are you making this personal? It's not about the woman, is it?"

Shifting in his seat, Reece swallowed hard and forced a level gaze. "You know me better than that."

"I thought I did. But you're spending way too much time worrying about this. We both know that computer and stereo are long-gone. I think it's time to close this investigation and move on. I could use you on a couple of other cases."

The thought of reducing Denni's case to one of hundreds stuffed unsolved into a filing cabinet sent shards of anger through Reece. With a tenacity he'd rarely used with his superior, he stood and leaned forward on his clenched fists. "I'm not ready to throw in the towel on this one, Chief. Trust me and give me a little more time."

Obviously not intimidated, the chief drummed his fingers over the open file. Reece held his breath while the man made up his mind. Finally after what seemed like an eternity, he glanced up and nodded. "I'll give it one more month. But you'll have to take on the Stuart case as well."

The thought of adding more work to his schedule didn't exactly thrill Reece, but he *was* thrilled with the permission to continue to work on Denni's case.

He walked out of the office with a lift in his spirits.

"I guess the chief didn't pull the plug after all, huh?" Sean came from behind and fell into step beside Reece. The kid had become his virtual shadow since his self-appointed decision to join the "hunt" for Denni's saboteur.

"I have a month."

"You mean *we* have a month." Sean chomped spearmint gum and fairly shook with pent-up energy.

"You're not even assigned to this case. What's in it for you?"

Sean shrugged. "I've seen Leigh somewhere. But every time I get this close to remembering, it leaves my mind. She doesn't have a record."

"You checked?"

"Yep. Not a thing on her."

Reece had already done that of course, but it irked him that Sean was playing lover boy to her face and investigating her behind her back. Leigh was a pain, but did she deserve that? Furthermore, was he any different in his dealings with Denni?

His mind went to the shared kiss. The feel of her, soft and pliable in his arms. His heart sped up at the memory. Why was it that when he finally found a woman he could picture a future with, she turned out to be religious? If there was a God, this was a nice little joke He was playing.

"So?"

The sound of his shadow's voice swung Reece back to the present. "So what?"

"Where do we go from here?"

"What do you mean?"

"After the fire the other night, I figure whoever is doing these things is probably stepping up the action. Right? It hasn't been that long since the flooded basement. So we might not have much time to catch her before she hurts someone."

"You really think it's Leigh?"

A troubled frown played at Sean's brow. "She doesn't seem like the type and if I had to guess, I'd say she loves Denni like a mom or something. But you're the one who told me not to assume anything. And not to let personal feelings distract me from doing a thorough investigation."

Reece nodded.

"If I could just figure out why Leigh looks so familiar, I could put it to rest or confirm that she's the one."

They walked out the double doors of the police station. Sean followed as Reece headed toward his Avalanche.

"Don't you have something to do?" Reece asked.

"Nope. Day off."

"Then what were you doing at the station?"

Sean shrugged and grinned, smacking his gum with perfectly white, straight teeth. "I like it. Besides I wanted to see what you were doing."

The kid reminded Reece of himself at that age. He remembered himself as a rookie cop, wide-eyed and determined to be a crackerjack. He'd pretty much achieved that goal. He supposed Sean would too. He was willing to use whatever means were necessary to solve a case.

"Get in."

"Where we going?"

"Where do you think?"

"I knew I should have worn my cologne. You wouldn't want to swing by my apartment would you?"

"Forget it, pretty boy. I don't think it's your fancy smell that makes Leigh's heart go pitter-patter, anyway."

"So, you think she really likes me?"

Reece rolled his eyes. "I don't know, Beav. Why don't you write her a note and ask her?"

Rather than being miffed by the sarcasm, Sean guffawed, slapping his crossed knee. "I think she does. I'm starting to hope she's not guilty."

"Really? You're rethinking taking her home to the folks?"

Sean shrugged. "They'd have to get used to her. I did. Once you look past the dark makeup and the piercings, she's a pretty great girl."

"Yeah, but how do you get past the fact that she can beat you up?" Reece snickered at his own joke.

"I'll just be nice to her so she doesn't have a reason to."

He had to hand it to the kid. He could take a little ribbing.

"Do you know she's carrying a 4.0 grade average? Has been since she started college, and she graduates in a few days, a full semester early. She got a full ride to the university. She was Denni's first girl. That's why she's older. She holds down a full-time job too. I think my parents would look at that part of her and the rest would just fade into the background in importance. Don't you think?"

"How do I know? I've never met your parents."

"What do you think yours would have done?"

Reece glared at him. This was starting to get too personal. "I never liked a girl enough to want to introduce her to family."

"Never? How old are you?"

"Drop it. I don't talk about my personal life with rookies."

Sean shrugged. "I just don't see how someone can get to be pushing what…senior citizenship? And never have been in love with a woman."

Denni stared at the woman standing on her porch. "Elizabeth. This is…quite a surprise."

"I'm sorry to barge in on you this way." The woman's tight-lipped smile failed to communicate any apology.

"Not at all," Denni said stepping aside. "Come in, please."

Elizabeth seemed ill at ease as she entered the house. She cleared her throat.

"What can I do for you?" Denni asked, closing the door.

"I think we need to discuss a concern I have about your application."

"Oh?" Denni immediately went on the defensive. "I'm sorry. It will be there soon."

"No, it's not that." Elizabeth glanced about the room as though assuring herself that no one could overhear. "My concern lies in the fact that your home seems to be run more like a foster home than a ministry."

Stinging under the criticism, Denni fought against the rising anger. "Elizabeth, I'm not sure what you mean. The girls are in church every time the doors are open."

"True. But other than that, what are you offering them that ensures their spiritual life?"

"I'm not sure what you're getting at."

Gathering a deep breath, Elizabeth met her gaze. "The girls come and go as they please."

Outrage filled Denni. She scowled. "I take it you've been talking to Mrs. James."

Elizabeth confirmed Denni's words by breaking eye contact.

Denni folded her arms across her chest, fully aware that the body language conveyed a woman on the defensive. "Let me assure you, Elizabeth, that the girls have a strict curfew when they are not working. But aside from that, they are adults, not children. They adhere to the house rules, attend church services, and that's good enough for me."

"That may be." Elizabeth fixed her with a frank stare. "But you are asking ministries to fund you from our ministry outreach funds. From the looks of things, what sets you apart from a foster home?" She reached into her bag and pulled out some brochures. "These are some ministries similar to what I believe you want to accomplish here. You might find some of the information useful. There are also phone numbers and Websites listed."

Denni opened her mouth to protest, then thought better of it. She nodded. "All right. I see your point. Let me look through these and pray and see what I can come up with to integrate more ministry tools into the house project, and I'll get it back to you with the application."

Elizabeth's face relaxed. "I look forward to reviewing it. Please do be sure to get it in soon. Time is running extremely short."

Feeling as though perhaps she'd found a sort of rapport with Elizabeth, Denni took a chance. "Would you like to come into the living room and have a cup of coffee? I'm afraid the kitchen is still a bit of a mess."

Elizabeth's guard shot back up. "No, thank you. I have to get back to the church."

Denni walked with her to the door. They stepped onto the porch just as Reece's Avalanche pulled into the drive.

Not again. Not again.

A person couldn't turn around without the detective snooping. How was she ever going to finish her plans for Denni if there were always cops about Mahoney House? Mother would blame her if something wasn't done soon. Apparently, drastic measures were going to have to be taken.

Denni stood on the porch until Reece and Sean reached her. "What brings the two of you over here?"

"We came to see if we could help with anything."

"Help?" Elizabeth's brow rose.

Denni smiled. "They've been helping with some repairs around the house."

Elizabeth nodded. "It's kind of you to offer to help, detective."

Denni couldn't tell if she was sincere or not.

The woman gave a tight smile. "Anyway, thank you for your time and I'll look forward to hearing from you." With a clipped nod, she moved across the porch, her heels clacking against the boards.

Reece and Sean moved aside as she walked down the steps. Reece cast a questioning glance at Denni. She shook her head, and pressed her lips together until Elizabeth was safely out of earshot.

"What was she doing here?" Reece asked.

"She came by to drop off some brochures from some benevolence ministries. She thought I might need to change the structure of Mahoney House a little."

A frown creased his brow. "Is she giving you a hard time?"

"I really don't know. She didn't seem confrontational this time. It was like a 'help me help you' sort of thing."

"I see." But he didn't sound convinced.

"Anyway," she said, "Don't you have to work today?" she asked.

"I took the rest of the day off." Reece smiled. "I'm all yours if you want me."

The implication of his statement made her breath shorten. But his eyes were innocent, so she forced herself not to read too much into his words. "I could use a couple of muscle men to move furniture. Think you can handle it?"

Sean grinned and flexed his biceps. "Bring it on."

For the next three hours, they worked, cleaning behind couches, chairs, bookcases, the china cabinet. They washed walls and knickknacks. Denni put the young people to work cleaning windows, upstairs and down. By the time she proclaimed a halt to the day's labor, the group descended, exhausted, upon the living room. They sprawled on newly shampooed and therefore slightly damp couches and carpet, but no one seemed to mind.

Reece sat next to Denni on the couch. He turned to her and her heart leaped into her throat at his smile.

"You know how to work a group."

"I was always in charge of spring-cleaning, growing up. My mother had very little structure to her life, but she insisted on a thorough cleaning every spring and fall."

"I'm starving," Cate piped up. The girl, now eight and a half months pregnant, looked about ready to explode. Denni had spared her most of the work, but she'd insisted on helping where she could.

Denni roused. "I guess I'll go rustle up some grub," she said in her best Old West accent.

Reece caught her fingers in his and pulled her back. Alarm shot through her as she over-compensated for the force and landed so close she was almost sitting on his lap. She ended up against his chest, her face a mere inch from his. "What are you doing?" she demanded, trying to add *oomph* to her voice, but finding the words difficult to get out in any tone.

"You're not cooking," he said. "I'd like to take you out."

"What about the rest of them?"

"We'll all go out," Sean suggested.

Reece scowled. Denni's heart thrilled. A group date obviously wasn't what he had in mind. "Next time it's just the two of us," he muttered, loud enough for her ears alone.

She tossed him a cheeky grin. "All right. We'll all go to Ramsey's. Leigh can get us a discount."

"No!" Leigh's protest rang into the room.

"I know, Leigh." Denni searched the girl's face. "I was only teasing about the discount." Leigh had worked at Ramsey's Barbecue Shack for the four years she'd been living with Denni.

"Sorry to overreact," she muttered. "I'm just so sick of barbecue." Her face had drained of color over the exchange. Denni made a mental note to seek her out later and talk about what was bothering her.

"No problem. We'll go out for seafood." Denni glanced around the room. "Anyone have a problem with that?"

She glanced at Reece for confirmation, but his sharp gaze rested on Leigh. Denni's stomach sank. She knew that look. Leigh's outburst had put her back at the top of his list.

Chapter Twelve

At the sound of the running motor in the driveway, Denni flung open the door, unable to contain the thrill of expectancy creeping through her. She'd spent all day putting together one outfit after another until she finally felt reasonably confident about the khaki capris and a black pullover top that hit the pants just below the waistband.

Black sandals, borrowed from an insistent Cate, bit the area between her big toe and the one next to it and she knew she'd have a fat blister by the time she got home. But no amount of complaining softened Cate's stance on the matter. "Blisters are a small price to pay for beauty," the girl insisted.

Reece was fifteen minutes late. After finally pulling an agreement from her to go out to dinner...just the two of them. As friends. So she'd expected to see his gray-and-black truck when she opened the door. Instead, a white sedan sat there mocking her.

Feeling as though someone had let all the air out of her tires, Denni stood in the doorway looking out at the beaming faces of her dad and his flamboyant bottle-blond fiancée, Ruth. They stood on the porch, luggage in hand, wearing matching Hawaiian shirts and identical grins.

Think, Denni! Had she forgotten they were coming to visit? She searched her overloaded brain for some morsel of memory to indicate she should be expecting them. Nothing.

"Surprise!" Even her wide-brimmed straw hat couldn't shade the excitement radiating from Ruth's overly made-up face.

Despite her bewilderment, Denni couldn't help but return the smile. Ruth dropped her suitcase and pulled Denni into a fierce embrace.

"Why didn't you two tell me you were coming?" Denni locked eyes with her dad and asked the question over Ruth's shoulder.

"That wouldn't have been much of a surprise, would it?" Her dad chuckled, and Denni moved from Ruth's arms to his.

"I suppose not." Denni plastered a fake smile on her face and gave herself an inward little pep talk about grace under fire. She hated surprises. She'd had enough of them lately to fill a lifetime.

A cloud of uncertainty flickered across Ruth's eyes. "Is this a bad time, honey? We don't have to stay. It's only an hour's drive home. Maybe we shouldn't have dropped in on you this way."

"No, of course not. It's just a surprise, that's all. And that was the whole point, wasn't it?"

Denni gave her a reassuring squeeze and snatched up the suitcase from where Ruth had dropped it. "Come inside." She opened the door wider, relieved beyond measure that spring-cleaning was out of the way and the house sparkled. The new stove had arrived a few days ago, and just yesterday Denni had finished painting the new wall behind the counter. So at least she wouldn't have to explain a burnt kitchen.

"How long are you planning to stay?"

"Through your birthday at least. Your dad, here, insists you can't spend your thirty-third birthday without family."

Her thirty-third…? For crying out loud, she'd forgotten all about that. Today was what? May tenth? And her birthday was the twelfth. Okay. Two or three days was doable. Now, if only the household could go a few days without a disaster, maybe Denni could keep up her facade that she had everything together.

Her mind instantly swung into plan-B mode, and she started organizing. Every available bed was spoken for, so Ruth would have to bunk with her. After Keri's complaints about their future stepmother's wild sleeping habits last Thanksgiving at the cabin, Denni wasn't too thrilled with the idea of sharing with the nocturnal gymnast.

"So, when are you two going to set a date?" she asked.

"You'll have to ask your dad that one, honey," Ruth said, casting a sidelong glance at Mac.

He scowled and Denni bit back her grin.

"We'll decide all that in good time. No sense in hurrying."

"Ha! You aren't exactly getting any younger," Ruth shot back. "Even if you are getting handsomer by the day."

Dad grinned and winked at his fiancée. He turned to Denni. "We'll be tying the knot before long."

Ruth sighed and locked her gaze with Mac's. The sight and sound of a woman emphatically in love made Denni uncomfortable, and she almost wished she hadn't diverted attention to that particular subject.

Ruth spared her the necessity of changing the subject again. The woman stood in the middle of the room hands on her hips, and looked around, a frown creasing her makeup. "Everything's looking pretty good to me. You'd never know you've had such trouble."

"Ruthie!"

At Dad's admonishment, Ruth's eyes grew wide, and her hand flew to her mouth.

Suspicion shot through Denni. She narrowed her gaze. "Never know about what trouble?"

Dad scowled and shook his head. "Women..."

"Never mind all that," Denni said firmly. "What is it that you know?"

"I'm not saying a word. We promised Keri we wouldn't spill anything."

"Let me guess. She told you about the problems I've been having around here."

Mac stepped forward and slid his arm around Denni's shoulders. "It's no more than you should have done from the very first incident. Daughters are supposed to let their dads in on problems like this. Especially if they don't have a husband to protect them."

A sigh whooshed from Denni's lungs. She could have done without the non-husband comment, but otherwise, relief washed over her as she leaned into the warm comfort of her dad's embrace. "I know, Dad. But I didn't want to worry anyone about a bunch of accidents."

"Accidents, my eye," Ruth said with a snort. "Honey, you've got to wake up and smell the coffee. Sure as I'm not a natural blonde, someone is out to shut you down."

That was the last time she'd tell her sister anything. All she needed was three days of "you should do this, and you should do that" coming from Dad and Ruth.

Pulling out of Dad's arms, she looked from one to the other. "How about some coffee? I just put on some fresh right before you got here," she said, hoping they'd take a hint and drop it for now.

No such luck.

"Now, don't go changing the subject," Dad broke in, his green eyes narrowing, accepting no nonsense from her.

Denni returned his scowl. She gave a shrug, feeling like a rebellious teen. "What do you want me to say?"

"You can start by admitting the truth of what's going on around here."

"I don't know what's going on, and I couldn't control it if I did know. So far I just take what comes, and quite frankly, every single incident, except for the theft, can easily be explained as an accident."

Dad raised his eyebrow. Only one. The dreaded single-eyebrow lift could mean only one thing: he wasn't buying it. "Do you want to explain to me how someone could turn on the water by accident? You either turn the knob or you don't. There is no *accidentally* to it."

"Okay, maybe *that* one wasn't an accident," Denni muttered. "But the kitchen fire was."

"You had another fire?" Ruth's gasp rang through the room like the bells at Notre Dame. "Keri only told us about the one in the laundry room."

Denni closed her eyes and inwardly moaned. She had to start writing down what she did and didn't tell which sister. Now she remembered. Raven had been on the phone the night of the fire. She'd called back later. That's why she knew about it. Denni had told her not to tell anyone. Bless her; she must have actually kept her mouth shut. Of course, when it came to family ties, Raven's rope was a bit thin, so she probably wouldn't have told them anyway.

"One of the girls accidentally left the burner on under a teapot and it caught fire."

"Was anyone hurt?" Ruth asked, her pale-blue eyes clouded with worry.

"No. We caught it in time. The damage was minimal and covered by insurance."

"That's a mercy."

"Yes."

"What do the police have to say about all of this?"

Denni had anticipated the question from her ex-cop dad. But she dreaded having to tell him the truth.

"Reece is still looking into the theft. But there's not much hope of getting the stuff back. I've already turned that in on the insurance, too."

"Who is this Reece?" Dad's sharp eyes raked her face for answers. Denni felt warmth creep to her cheeks.

"Detective Corrigan, rather," she said, even though she knew it was too late to cover up her attraction to him. Ruth's knowing smile spoke volumes.

Apparently, Dad was too focused on the questions to worry about the implications. "Does Corrigan have any leads on the fires and flooding incidents?"

"Well, no, I…"

"After all this time? What have they been doing down at that police station while my daughter's in danger?"

"Remember your blood pressure, sweetie," Ruth reminded him softly.

Denni watched her Dad's face instantly relax at the sound of his fiancée's voice. She marveled at the love he had found with the elderly Southern belle. Ruth was a lucky woman. Denni remembered her own mother's voice having the same effect on her dad when his Irish temper rose.

A wave of longing for her mother washed over Denni. What might it have been like to have her mother sitting in her living room, with Denni pouring out her worry over the funding for the houses and her growing feelings for Reece, a man who was clearly not suited to her? Just to shift the burden of responsibility if only for a few minutes.

Oh, Mama. I miss you.

Suddenly aware of her dad and Ruth's presence, Denni shook off the gloom. "In response to your question," Denni said. "I haven't issued a report for any of them. The fire in the laundry room was contained in the trash can. Luckily, Leigh found it and put it out before it did much more than smoke up the room. I never reported the flooded basement, and the fire investigator officially concluded that the kitchen fire was an accident."

Dad gave an old-fashioned Irish snort. "That's a bunch of blarney. And you're as aware of it as I am, little girl. There were no accidents here. I want that detective's name and the number of the police station. Or better yet, I'll go down there myself."

The doorbell rang as if by design.

Denni rolled her eyes. "You won't have to go down there. That's Reece." And only thirty minutes late.

Reece stared across the kitchen table into the wizened old eyes of Mac Mahoney and felt suddenly like a rookie cop. No, worse, he felt like Denni's prom date getting the third degree about where to keep his hands.

He rubbed his damp palms on the front of his jeans for the third time. He gulped and couldn't keep himself from addressing Mr. Mahoney as sir.

Denni seemed more than a little amused at his discomfiture, but at the same time, Reece could feel her own tension.

"I have several leads," he admitted, not wanting to upset Denni, but feeling the need to reassure her dad, nonetheless, before he hotfooted down to the station and made a big scene. The less attention brought to the case in front of the chief, the better as far as Reece was concerned. It would be best if the chief could sort of forget about the case until Reece was ready to offer him up a credible suspect, complete with Miranda rights and handcuffs.

"What sorts of leads do you have?"

Denni gave a short laugh. "He's hot on the trail of a houseful of college-aged girls. And one of them is eight and a half months pregnant. She couldn't have bent over to turn on that water faucet if her life depended on it. She can't even tie her own shoes anymore."

"Oh, dear," Ruth remarked, obviously either ignoring Denni's sarcasm or not catching it to begin with. "Do you really think one of Denni's girls is the culprit?"

Before Reece could respond, Denni stood up. "Oh, wait. He has another suspect…my next door neighbor. Just because she's a little leery of the girls."

Mac nodded. "That seems likely."

"She's eighty years old!" Denni exploded. "It's ridiculous even to suggest such a thing. Mrs. James is cantankerous and nosy, but that doesn't mean she'd do anything illegal to get rid of us. Oh but wait. Let's take the heat off of her. After all, she does have a fifty-year-old daughter who is a…what did you call her? A nutcase?"

"I said she was nuts, but that's beside the point. We have to consider all possible suspects, or don't you want to solve these incidents?"

"Nosiness doesn't constitute guilt."

Reece glared at her. "I know her nosiness doesn't mean she's guilty, but I'm still investigating. And I don't care if she's eighty or a hundred and eighty, if I find out she's responsible, I'll arrest her."

"And her little dog too?" Sarcasm rolled the words from Denni's tongue.

Irritation shot into his stomach and grew to frustration. "You saying I'm acting like the Wicked Witch of the West? I'm trying to save your project. All I get is resistance. What's wrong with you?"

"Here, now." Mac leaned forward in his chair. "No sense raising your voices."

Reece glanced back to Denni's dad. "I'm sorry. But she's so stubborn. I can't make her admit for one second that one of those girls could have done those things."

"Well, the theft, maybe," Mac said. "But why try to ruin the house? They wouldn't have anywhere to live."

"Exactly." Denni's head nodded with her statement as she jumped on her dad's support.

"I agree. And that's where Mrs. James comes in."

"An eighty-year-old woman?" Mr. Mahoney's fiancée sent him a you-should-be-ashamed-of-yourself look.

Warmth crept up Reece's neck. "I know it doesn't seem likely, but she does have motive. She absolutely hates the girls."

"*Hate* is a pretty strong word," Denni said. "Mrs. James hasn't quite been won over yet, but I think it's just a matter of time."

Reece shook his head at her infernal optimism. "What are you going to do, Pollyanna? Bake her a pie?"

Mac snorted in amusement.

Denni glared at them both. "I'm going to 'love my neighbor' like the Bible says, and trust God to make 'even my enemies be at peace with me.'"

"Good for you!" Ruth slapped her palm on the oak tabletop. "How's that for taking the Word and applying it to life?"

Fighting the urge to roll his eyes, Reece looked to Mac for support. The man shrugged. "Sure, honey," he said and Reece wasn't sure which of the women present *honey* referred to. "But the Word also says to be 'wise as a serpent.'"

Oh, brother. It ran in the family. All he'd wanted to do was take Denni out for a nice dinner. Maybe stroll through the public gardens, and if the mood was right, kiss her in the moonlight. How had those plans gotten so messed up? He sure hadn't banked on sitting at the table being grilled like a teenaged kid and getting a Bible lesson at the same time.

"I'm not burying my head in the sand, Dad. Someone is out to stop us. I can admit to that."

Now they were getting somewhere. Reece waited for her to go on.

"But these girls…" Her voice faltered and tears misted her eyes. That chivalrous guy Reece hadn't known was buried in his chest until he'd met Denni rose to the surface again, nudging him to reach over and take her hand. He resisted the urge as she continued. "…these girls and I, we're like family. They wouldn't do anything to hurt me. Any more than I'd hurt one of them. It's not like I'm an authority figure that has to be avoided or bested. We're in this for the long haul. If it fails or succeeds, we're sticking together and we'll make it. Even if I have to go back to work full-time."

"What about when you get married? I don't see a guy agreeing to an arrangement where he has to share his wife with a bunch of girls."

Reece immediately regretted his words as all three sets of eyes stared at him: Mac, with a confused frown that clearly wondered what difference that made when his daughter might be living with a whacko out to hurt her, Ruth with a big Texas-style grin that didn't hold back what she was thinking, and Denni…he couldn't quite decipher her expression. He cleared his throat. "Never mind. It doesn't matter."

"Denni? I thought you had a date…oh." Denni glanced up to find Cate standing in the door. "Sorry," she muttered. "I've interrupted. I didn't know you had guests."

Ruth jumped to her feet and marched straight over to the girl. "Honey, you look about ready to pop any second. I'd say that bun is just about baked, wouldn't you?" She took her by the shoulders. "Now, you come right on in here and take a load off those swollen ankles. I'm going to get you a nice cool glass of milk."

Bewilderment lit Cate's eyes and she stared at Denni with a who's-this-nutso? look.

Denni smiled. "Cate, you remember my dad, don't you? And this is my stepmother-to-be-if-dad-ever-gets-around-to-it, Ruth."

Mac stood and extended his hand. "Nice to see you again." His gaze swept over her protruding middle. "You'd best sit down like Ruthie suggested."

Cate sat. Whether she wanted to or not.

Reece stood, figuring now was as good a time as any to make his exit since his date with Denni was pretty much ruined. "I guess I'll be shoving off now. It was nice to meet you, Mr. Mahoney and Ms.—"

Ruth set a tall glass of milk on the table in front of Cate. The older woman glanced up at Reece. "Call me Ruth. Everyone does. But you can't leave. You and Denni had plans. Don't let us interrupt those plans. Mac and I can stay here and get acquainted with Cate and whoever else is home tonight. Right, Cate?"

The girl swallowed hard enough so that Reece could hear the milk go down with difficulty. "Yes, ma'am," she whispered.

Denni came to her rescue. "Don't be silly. I'll order pizza, and Reece can stay and have dinner here with us."

She gave him a pleading glance, silently begging him to back her up. Realization struck him that, unless he agreed to the new development, Denni would be forced to leave her girls at the mercy of an overbearingly motherly woman and a man they didn't know.

He was tempted to take Ruth up on her first offer and whisk Denni away. Let the girls hold their own. But looking into Denni's gorgeous eyes, he abandoned the idea as quickly as it flashed through his mind and surrendered like a purring cat.

"Pizza sounds great. Just what I had in mind."

Chapter Thirteen

Denni's heart nearly stopped when her hand brushed against Reece's as they each reached for the last slice of pizza. Her cheeks warmed and she pulled back. Reece lifted the slice and dropped it onto her plate. "Never let it be said I'm not a gentleman," he said with a grin.

"How sweet," Ruth said. Denni wished her dad would hurry up and marry the woman so she'd lose that starry-eyed approach to every situation. Didn't she realize that only a jerk would take the last piece of pizza? Reece knew that and didn't want to make a bad impression. That was *all* there was to read into that event.

She took her knife and halved the slice. "Here, I'll share. That many fewer calories I have to worry about."

Did Ruth just heave a blissful sigh? Reece's chuckle confirmed that she had. Silently, Denni choked down the last of her food, wishing she'd obeyed her full stomach in the first place and not yielded to the tempting last slice.

She glanced around the table, happy that so many of the girls were home tonight. Only Leigh had had to work.

They were getting used to Reece's presence at the house and conversation was lively. Not stilted and suspicious as it had been the first few times Reece had shared a meal with them. Denni wasn't so sure it was necessarily a good thing that they were relaxing when he was around. The whole thing reminded her of coaxing a dog with a bone just so you could catch it and pen it up.

The thought made her uncomfortable, because if Reece was playing the girls, he was most likely playing her as well. And if that was the case, then the most spectacular kiss of her life meant little or nothing to the man who had shared it with her.

Unable to sit there another minute thinking about the implications of his likely deceit, she stood and began to gather up the dishes. "Oh, no you don't." Denni glanced up in surprise as Ruth snatched the stack of plates from her hand. "Mac and I are doing dishes tonight," the woman said. "No arguments."

Denni couldn't help but be amused at the scowl on her dad's face. Dishes weren't exactly his thing. He loved to cook, but always left clean-up to anyone else. But he looked from Ruth to Denni and then to Reece and nodded. "All right. I'll help."

"Me too," Cate offered.

"Honey, you better go lay down for awhile." Ruth's motherly gaze rested on Cate's weary face. "You need to save up all your strength for labor."

Cate's face grew pink, but she nodded and lumbered to her feet. According to her due date, she had two more weeks to go, but Denni didn't see how she could possibly last that long.

The phone beeped and Fran answered. "It's for you, Denni," she said handing the cordless over.

Denni walked from the crowded kitchen into the living room. "Hello?" She plopped down on the sofa.

"Hello, this is Elizabeth Wilson."

"Elizabeth?" What on earth could she be calling about? "Working late?" Denni asked, keeping her tone friendly despite the chill coming through the phone line.

"Yes. We're going over grant applications. Pastor asked me to call and remind you that tomorrow is the deadline." Elizabeth's tight voice held no warmth whatsoever. But Denni was determined not to let that affect her own response.

"Thank you for calling, Elizabeth. Please tell him that I mailed it off yesterday."

"I've got to have it by tomorrow's deadline or I'll be forced to choose another charity for next year."

"I understand," Denni replied. "If it didn't get there today, it should by no later than tomorrow. It didn't really have that far to go."

"Yes, well. Provided it was indeed mailed, it should arrive by tomorrow, then. But if it *doesn't* arrive, we can't treat you with any sort of favoritism."

Denni bristled at the continued animosity. Was Elizabeth calling her a liar?

"Look, I don't know why you would think I didn't mail it when I said I did, but I assure you I wouldn't take a chance on missing out on funding from my own church."

"You seem to be pretty certain of the outcome for your little project. There are no guarantees even if I do receive it tomorrow." The tension in Elizabeth's voice had somehow switched from cool professionalism to anger in midsentence. "Don't get your hopes up. Remember, I have a large influence over who receives funding."

The phone clicked on the other end, leaving Denni to listen to dead air. Elizabeth had actually hung up on her. Unease crept through Denni. Five years was an awfully long time to hold a grudge. She pressed the button to turn off the phone.

"You didn't say goodbye to whoever you were talking to."

Denni jumped at the sound of Reece's voice. She jerked her chin up to face him. "You shouldn't sneak up on people like that."

He smiled. "Sorry. Occupational hazard."

"It's okay. Want to sit down?"

Reece crossed the room and filled the space at the other end of the couch, turning his body slightly so that he faced Denni.

"That was Elizabeth Wilson reminding me that tomorrow is the deadline date for my application. I didn't say goodbye because she hung up on me."

"Why'd she do that?"

Denni shrugged. "She thinks I am assuming that I'll get the grant. I guess it irks her."

"Is there any reason to assume you *won't* get it?" Absently, he rubbed his index finger over the soft fabric of the couch. "I mean did you do anything they didn't like with the money from last year?"

"Not that I know of. But this is the first year Elizabeth has been in charge of making recommendations to the committee."

"And that's relevant because?"

Was it her imagination, or did Reece seem more than casually interested? That look in his eyes was familiar. He was prowling. She fought the irritation rising in her chest.

Why did everything have to be about the investigation with him? Couldn't he just listen to her and not make it about floods, fires and thefts? "Because she doesn't like me. A few years ago I had to turn her down as a foster parent. If she recommends that I do not get a grant, it's unlikely I will."

"Isn't that a little unusual?"

"What?"

"Turning people down in a state woefully short on homes for kids?"

She searched his face carefully. The look he gave her in return was way too innocent. Reece might be a crackerjack detective, but he was a lousy actor. He knew something about the history between Elizabeth and Denni, but he was trying really hard not to show it.

Admittedly, Elizabeth *could* be a suspect. Denni's heart sank. If the woman was behind all this, Denni had no chance at all of getting the grant.

Reece tried to remain coolly disinterested, but by the slant of Denni's eyes, he could see that he'd blown it. She knew something was up.

"Corrigan, what's your interest in Elizabeth?"

Reece sent her a sheepish grin. "All right. I was hoping you'd just tell me. But I'll confess. I know all about Elizabeth's drug arrest and the state turning her down as a foster mother. I also know you're the one who had to break the news to her."

With a growl, she rocketed up from the couch. "Why can't we have one single conversation without you having to make it into something about the case?"

"Because we can't move forward with us until your case is solved."

Move forward? Reece caught himself. Moving forward—what was he talking about?

Obviously, Denni's mind was mulling over the same questions. She stared at him, waiting for him to continue. Her mouth opened just enough to soften her lips and make Reece sweat. If she didn't stop looking at him like that…

"Hey, what's all the hollerin' about in here?"

Nothing like the sight of a girl's dad to douse the flames. Denni gave a sigh and faced Mac. "Nothing, Dad. Reece and I were just talking about the case."

"Ahh, that explains the noise."

"Yeah." Her face showed a war of emotions.

A vibration coming from the cell phone hooked to Reece's waistband alerted him to yet another call. He'd ignored all the vibrations during dinner, but now was probably a good time to go ahead and take a call. He stood and lifted his phone from his belt. The caller ID showed it was the police station.

"Excuse me," he said to include Denni and Mac. "I have to take this." He pressed the button. "Hello?"

"Hey Reece."

Reece frowned. The kid. What was Sean doing calling him during Reece's off hours? For that matter, how had he finagled Reece's number? His number was not to be given out, especially to rookies. Someone's head was going to roll.

"Are you still with Denni?" Sean asked.

Reece glanced at Denni. Her cheeks darkened as she realized she'd been caught listening in. He winked, enjoying that her blush deepened. She turned and left the room. Mac followed, leaving Reece alone in the living room.

"That's right," he said into the receiver. "Hang on." He walked toward the door and stepped outside, onto the porch. "Okay, I can talk now. What do you want?"

"I figured out where I've seen Leigh before."

"Is it relevant?"

"I don't know. Maybe."

"Okay. Let's hear it."

"I'm working tonight and a call came in from the Glass Slipper."

Reece's gut tightened with dread. Surely Leigh wasn't...

"Brandt and I headed over there to break up a pretty big fight. And then I saw her."

Reece groaned. "Dancing?"

"Actually, she was in the middle of the fight," Sean said glumly. "A guy had tried to do more than watch her dance, and she hit him over the head with a bottle."

"In the weeks you two have been dating, she didn't bother to let you in on the minor news that she's a stripper?"

"Guess not. And she's not apologizing."

No, Reece didn't figure she'd be the type.

"But remember how I thought she looked familiar?" Sean said. "I've broken up fights at the Glass Slipper before."

"Sorry, Sean."

"Anyway," Sean said. "Is there any way you can come down here and get her? She needs a ride back to her car, and I can't get away from here."

Picking up Leigh was about the last thing Reece wanted to do with the remainder of his evening. But the poor rookie sounded so blindsided by tonight's event that he didn't have the heart to suggest putting the girl in a cab.

"All right. I'll do it, but I have to say goodbye to Denni, first."

"Thanks, Reece. I owe you one."

"Nah, call us even. You've helped me out a lot lately."

"One more thing. Maybe you shouldn't say anything to Denni about this. Leigh might get kicked out of the house if Denni knows about the stripping."

After disconnecting the call, Reece went back inside. He found Denni in the kitchen, sitting at the table with a mug of coffee.

"Duty calls," he said with a smile.

Denni nodded and stood. "I'll walk you out."

He said his goodbyes to Ruth and Mac and snatched Denni's hand once they reached the living room. He laced his fingers with hers and led her onto the porch. The dusky night smelled of freshly cut grass, and cicadas broke the stillness of the quiet street with their grating call.

"I'm sorry to cut our night short," Reece said.

"It's all right."

Was it his imagination, or did she seemed relieved?

"About what I said earlier…" Reece swallowed hard. "I didn't mean to assume anything about our relationship."

Denni smiled. "Let's just take it one step at a time, okay?"

"I'd better go."

She nodded.

Unable to resist the temptation, he leaned forward and brushed her lips in a quick kiss. "I'll call you later."

"Okay," Denni replied softly, obviously caught off guard.

Reece hopped into his truck and sped off toward the police station. His attention shifted from Denni to

Leigh, and anger began to build. How could Leigh take Denni's kindness and then do something she knew would humiliate Denni if anyone found out? Not to mention the fact that it would break Denni's heart to discover Leigh was stripping in the first place.

So, if she was this good at keeping secrets, was she keeping others as well?

Maybe he'd been right about this one all along.

Chapter Fourteen

Reece's gut clenched at the sight of Leigh wrapped in a blanket. She leaned against a wall, staring at the waxed tile, trying to ignore the stares from a group of teen boys milling around the waiting area.

The sight of her crestfallen face touched something in Reece's heart. She looked as if she'd happily sink through the floor. "Leigh." He kept his voice soft. No use antagonizing her any more than her situation had already done. In a fair fight, Leigh was a worthy sparring partner in their verbal war, but her humiliation put her at a disadvantage. And Reece wasn't about to give in to the temptation to humiliate her further. There was no satisfaction in that.

Leigh's chin rose and her shoulders squared, her body language signaling she was more than ready for anything Reece wanted to dish out. Her lips curled into a mocking sneer.

"Save it, Corrigan."

"I'm here to take you back to your car."

She gave a short laugh. "Yeah, right. I'd rather walk."

Reece glanced down at the five-inch spikes on her shoes. "Okay, walk then."

A pair of the teen boys sauntered past, and sized her up and down. "How much for an hour, baby?"

Leigh came off the wall, fury blazing in her face. "What did you say to me, you little jerk?"

Grabbing hold of her arm before she could knock the tar out of the little runt, Reece fixed the teen with a sharp glare. "Do you want to be arrested for solicitation, punk?"

The kid's face blanched. "Just kidding."

Reece jerked his thumb at the pair. "Get out of here."

Leigh's face glowed red with what Reece assumed was a mixture of embarrassment and anger.

"Let's go," he said.

Leigh followed without a struggle. Once in his truck, she turned to him. "Don't say anything to Denni. You know what this would do to her."

"Not to mention that it'll get you kicked out of the house."

She snorted. "Forget it. Tell her whatever you want. I'm not begging you."

"Let's say, for instance, that I keep my mouth shut…"

He felt her shift, obviously listening, although she didn't respond.

"Are you going to stop dancing at the club?"

"Not that it's any of your business, but I got fired."

Relief shifted through Reece. "How long have you been doing it?"

"A few months."

Months. The girl was sneaky. Suspicion burned through him. Sneaky enough to rip off her benefactress and pretend to be the most caring of the bunch? Denni was too loyal to suspect her. But Reece wasn't about to let it go.

"What else are you hiding from Denni?"

"None of your business."

He stifled a growl. The girl was a closed book. Worse than that, she'd call his bluff at every turn without batting one of those fake eyelashes, just so he wouldn't have the satisfaction of seeing her cave. But there had to be a crack in her armor somewhere. And he was just the man to find it.

"Let me ask you this...how have you been able to keep Denni from finding out? I assume even the other girls don't know?"

"Only Shelley."

"Okay. So neither of you can be trusted."

"Hey. Just because I'm dancing so I can graduate from college doesn't mean I had anything to do with the stuff going on at the house." She slammed her fist against the dash and though he hated to admit it, Reece jumped. "Why can't you get off my back?"

"Why can't you graduate without taking off your clothes?"

It wasn't a fair comeback. Reece knew that. But his mind had zeroed in on that little comment and he had no intention of going another round with her about whether she did or didn't lift the computer and stereo from the house. Although a need to pay a tuition bill might explain things.

"My scholarship was cut off because I had to drop below half time last semester."

"Why?"

"Personal reasons."

"Does Denni know about that?"

"She knows part of it. And I don't intend that she find out the rest."

"Then come clean. Convince me you're not a thieving little user."

She heaved a sigh. "All right. This goes no further than this truck. Do you hear me?"

"Unless it's criminal, you have my word."

His words obviously touched a chord and she sent him a raking scowl. "I was dating this guy last year and I ended up pregnant." From the corner of his eye, Reece could see her scrutinizing his reaction. Years as a detective had taught him to remain coolly detached from shocking pieces of information. This was no different.

"So you got pregnant. Then what?"

"I had a miscarriage before I could even decide what I wanted to do. Abortion, adoption, keep it and be a decent mom." Reece recognized a crack in her shield. But only for a second. She shrugged. "Anyway. I got depressed, started using a little to feel better."

"So you dance to support your habit." He almost laughed. And he'd been starting to feel sorry for the little druggie.

"I quit using. And that's the part Denni knows about. She helped me check into a clinic. I don't have a problem anymore."

"Sure. Denial is the first indication you have a problem," he baited.

"Ask your little friends down at the bat cave, supercop." She sneered. "Do you think the cops would have let me go if I'd tested positive for drugs?"

She had a point there. "All right. So you stopped using."

"While I was using, I skipped too many classes. If I hadn't dropped out of one—which is what put me below half-time—I would have failed. I can't afford to have a failing grade on my record if I want to get into a decent med school.

"A friend of mine from school worked at the club to pay her way through school. So I hooked up with her."

"So, how have you managed to keep it from Denni for so long? I heard her call the barbecue shack the other night to check up on you."

"Yeah, that's a rule. She has to do periodic checks."

"So?"

"I worked there for a long time. They cover for me."

Reece whipped the truck into the parking lot of the Glass Slipper, hoping no one would recognize him.

"Look, Corrigan. I don't like lying to Denni. And believe me, if there was any other way, I'd have quit that rat hole of a job a long time ago."

"What are you going to do now? Find another place to dance?"

A heavy sigh escaped her. "No. I don't think so. Getting hauled down to the police station sort of cured me of that."

Reece nodded his approval. "Good for you. What then? You still have to pay for school."

A shrug lifted the slim shoulders. "I guess I'll have to work two jobs until next semester. I should be able to apply for loans by then."

"One question. Why didn't you just apply for the grants and loans already? Surely with your circumstances, you qualify."

"It was too late for this year. Next year is a different story. Until then, I have to do whatever it takes to stay in school."

The determination in her voice struck a familiar tone. And even after he watched her walk to her car and slip inside, he couldn't get the pleading out of his mind. Oh, Leigh had too much pride to ask for help in a blatant manner, but he recognized a cry for help when he heard one.

He'd given that same cry himself as a kid. He had just needed someone to believe in him. To give him a break so that he could better himself. Thomas and Lydia Ide had answered that call. Had given him the benefit of every doubt society in general had about him. They were that kind of people. But look where it had gotten them— dead. They had believed in all "their boys" and they were dead because of one kid who couldn't be saved.

Jonathon was locked up tighter than a nut in a shell. Fifty years to life for the double homicide. It was a good thing he'd turned eighteen a week before slicing their foster parents' throats while they slept, otherwise he might have ended up in juvie and been released a long time ago.

Reece's cell phone buzzed, effectively pulling him from the downward spiral of darkness that this line of thinking always led to. Reece sucked in a lungful of air and exhaled, pulling the phone from his belt.

"Yeah."

"Reece?"

Denni's sweet tone spread over him like warm oil, relieving the tension in his gut. "Hi, I'm glad you called."

"You are?" The surprise in her tone sent a shard of guilt through him. Did she really have to wonder how he felt about her?

"I'm more than glad."

"I'm happy to hear that. I was afraid having dinner with my dad and Ruth might have scared you off."

Not a chance. Her brand of spicy-sweetness had

wrapped him like a cozy, freshly washed comforter. And he had no desire to break free. He heard her hesitate, and he spoke up quickly, "What are you wearing?"

She gasped. Heat shot up the back of his neck like a fire updraft. "I'm not being perverted. Just wondering if you've already dressed for bed. I thought we might go out for coffee. I know an all-night doughnut shop."

"All right." Her simple acceptance of his invitation made his heart soar.

"I'll be there in ten minutes."

Denni sprang into action, slinging open her closet door. "Ten minutes, ten minutes!"

Where were her button-fly Levi's? Where were they?

Rissa! She had asked to borrow Denni's favorite jeans last week. She must not have returned them. "Rissa!"

She continued to riffle through the closet at breakneck speed. She could hear the sound of footsteps bounding up the stairs. Seconds later, the door flew open. "What's wrong?"

Dad stood, breathless, worry lines creasing his brow. Rissa peeked over his shoulder.

"Rissa, where are my jeans?"

"Jeans?" Disbelief flooded her face.

But Denni didn't care. Reece would be here in five minutes, and she needed those jeans!

"You mean to tell me you screamed bloody murder over a pair of britches?" Mac shook his head in disgust.

"Yes I did. Reece will be here in a couple of minutes to get me, and I need my jeans."

"What do you mean he's coming to get you?"

"That's wonderful, Denni, darlin'. Your jeans are in my closet. I'll just go get them."

"Oh, Mac," Ruth said, placing a gentle hand on his shoulder. "Leave her alone so she can get dressed. After all, it's our fault they had to cancel their date."

"Well, I don't think it's a very good idea for her to be going out this late."

"It's only ten o'clock." Ruth chuckled. "Come on let's go so she can get ready."

Cate and Fran wished Denni a nice time and wandered back to whatever they were doing before Denni's outburst. Shelley remained, her face twisted in disapproval. "Why are you going out with this guy, Denni? He's only dating you to try to pin the robbery and all the accidents on one of us."

Stung, Denni slowly nodded. "I guess that's possible, Shell." After all, what could he possibly see in the likes of her?

"I didn't mean it like that, Denni. You'd be a good catch for any lucky guy. I just mean that he's playing you. Don't fall for him."

"Here's the jeans." Rissa showed up at the door and tossed Denni the jeans. "Put them on. I'll get you a shirt." She stopped and surveyed their faces. "What's wrong?"

Shelley pushed past her, knocking against Rissa's shoulder. "Nothing."

"What was that all about?"

Denni slipped the jeans over her hips and sucked in to fasten all five buttons. "Shelley is concerned about Reece's motives."

Rissa tossed her a green pullover top with a V-neck and short-short sleeves. "Wear this. Green brings out the hazel in your eyes. His motives for what?"

"I'll freeze in that shirt."

"Take a jacket. Here." She handed her a faded denim jacket that exactly matched the jeans. "His motives for what?"

"Dating me." Denni shrugged into the jacket and surveyed her image in the full-length mirror on the inside of her closet door. Shelley was right. What *was* Reece's motive?

"Oh, Denni. Don't listen to her." Rissa slipped her arm about Denni's shoulders. "There are lots of reasons Reece, or any other guy for that matter, would want to spend time with you. Your gorgeous eyes and auburn hair are only two of those reasons. Your goodness balances out his suspicious nature. Sounds like a match made in heaven to me."

"No. It isn't. Reece isn't a Christian."

"Oh."

They both knew the implication of that. Denni made a face in the mirror. "What am I doing? I can't date Reece. Shelley's probably right, anyway."

"I don't know what's wrong with Shelley lately. But don't let her get to you." Rissa drew a deep breath. "As to dating Reece. That has to be your decision."

The doorbell chimed below. Rissa headed for the bedroom door. "I'll leave you alone."

Denni gave herself one more critical glance and grabbed her purse. She had only one real choice. Reece would have to understand that they could be friends, but nothing more. She would have coffee with him and break off any chance of romance between them.

Feeling right about her decision, she descended the stairs. He looked up when she walked into the living room. His eyes roamed over her, appreciation written on his face.

Denni's heart jumped.

Oh, Lord. Give me strength.

Chapter Fifteen

Staring into Denni's pale face and misty chocolate-brown eyes, Reece felt as though he'd been sucker-punched. Suddenly the warm doughnut on the table in front of him held no appeal and the one he'd already consumed sat anchored like a ball of lead in his stomach.

"You've got to be kidding. You'd really let something like religion stand in the way of whatever this thing is between us?"

"What exactly is this thing between us, Reece?"

He shrugged. Closing off his heart seemed to be the only sensible option considering she'd already made her intentions known. "Maybe nothing. Probably nothing."

Denni didn't look any happier than Reece felt. Reece could have kicked himself for allowing his heart to get involved. He knew better. He'd sort of known Christians didn't go for guys who didn't go to church, and still, he'd allowed himself to fall for this one-of-a-kind woman sitting across from him.

"I'm sorry, Reece." The misery covering her face

couldn't have been put on. "I blame myself for this. I shouldn't have encouraged your romantic attention."

Reece forced a casual tone and offered her a one-sided grin. "So, why did you?"

She searched his eyes as though trying to gauge just how much of his attitude was real and how much was put on. She knew him too well. Reece's gaze faltered before her scrutiny.

"I guess I enjoyed the attention." Her honesty took the wind right out of his sails and Reece found it impossible to hold a grudge. "All right. So, friends it is. How do we do that after all the kissing?"

Her cheeks pinked. "What do you mean all the kissing?" She grinned. "Either your kisses are completely forgettable or there have only been two."

Laughter rumbled deep in his throat. "You're feisty. I like that about you."

"You did the right thing, hon."

Ruth set a warm mug of hot chocolate on the table in front of Denni and patted her shoulder on the way to her own chair.

"I know," Denni returned, glumly. Her heart ached as much as if it had been on the losing end of a major fight. Battered and bruised. The force of her disappointment hung over her heavily. "It's really my own fault. I shouldn't have allowed myself to fall for him."

"The heart doesn't always give us a choice."

"I know. But God promises to make a way of escape. I shouldn't have let it go so far."

"How far did it go?"

Ruth's concerned frown struck a funny chord in Denni. She expelled a short laugh, cradling her mug between her palms. "Not too far, like that. Believe me; I'm still as pure as the driven snow."

The sarcasm in her own voice made her cringe. She was proud of her track record with men. Proud that God had kept her innocent. But after all...she was a grown woman. Definitely ready to settle into a relationship—marriage, children, happily-ever-after. That Reece! Why couldn't he just be a Christian?

Silence tensed the air and she glanced up, catching Ruth's questioning stare. "Don't mind me, Ruth. Every birthday since I turned twenty-three has been a depressing testament to the fact that I'm an old maid."

"Old maid? You're only thirty-three."

"Not until tomorrow." At least one more day.

"Tomorrow, then." Ruth smiled and sipped her decaf coffee. "Women are getting married a lot older now than they did in my day."

"Yeah." But her prospects were looking awfully thin. Besides, where would she ever find another man half as appealing as Reece Corrigan? Oh, it was just too depressing to even think about any more.

Her chair scraped against the linoleum as she moved back and stood. "It's almost midnight. I guess I'll go to bed."

Ruth smothered a yawn behind her veiny hand. "Me too, honey. I turn into a pumpkin in ten minutes. I'll just wash up these dishes lickety-split."

Denni made her rounds through the downstairs, turning off any overlooked lights. She paused in the living room and smiled fondly at the lump on the couch. Loving the nostalgia invading her senses, she listened for a minute to the sound of her dad snoring softly under the quilt.

Ruth joined her and the two women headed upstairs.

Denni's legs felt like petrified wood as she climbed. Just a few more steps and she could bury herself under the covers and try to sink into an oblivious sleep for at least six hours. Eight if she was lucky. Ten if they remembered it was her birthday.

Ruth followed her into the bedroom. Oh, yeah. So much for alone time.

She gave her future stepmother a gracious smile and waved toward the queen-size bed. "Which side do you want?"

If someone didn't turn off that alarm, Denni was going to go through the roof! There, it beeped again. She hadn't even set the stupid thing last night! Slowly, her world came into mental focus, the fog of night receded. The alarm sounded again. Denni frowned and opened one eye. That wasn't the alarm. It was her cell phone.

Unlike Raven's cultural ring, the no-nonsense beep-beep-beep ring belonged to her little sister, Keri. Their dad had ordered a nationwide family plan and had given each girl her own phone for Christmas. They'd had fun programming each other's phones with their preferred rings.

She fumbled on the nightstand for the beeping waker of sleeping birthday girls. "Hi Keri," she mumbled.

"Good morning, and happy birthday!" Her sister's perky voice lifted the morning blahs and coaxed a smile from Denni. She wiggled to a sitting position.

"What time is it?"

"Mmm. Ten o'clock. Are you seriously still in bed?"

"Surprisingly. They must have been tiptoeing around all morning. Ruth and Dad are here. Did you know that?"

"Yeah. Dad called before they left."

That reminded her... "What's the big idea telling

them about the accidents going on around here? I thought we had a deal?"

"Oh, come on, Denni." Keri's voice held not even a hint of remorse. "You know I can't keep something like that from Dad. Besides I think it's a good idea for him to look around and see what's going on there."

Denni rolled her eyes. "Cops," she said in mock disgust.

"Hey. Former cops. Dad's retired, and I'm now a proud co-director of the Kansas City inner-city mission and a mother to a couple of adorable ten-year-old twin sons."

Denni grinned and forgave. "How are Josh and Billy getting along in the new house?"

"They love it. Did I tell you Justin built them an enormous treehouse out back?"

"*Justin* did?"

"You say that like you doubt my man's abilities just a little bit." Her voice rang with mock offense.

"Not just a little doubt but highly, highly doubt," Denni returned wryly, not backing down. "I mean, like if my doubts were dollars, we'd be millionaires."

Keri laughed. "Okay, you're right. I'm lying. But he *did* supervise the building of said treehouse. And he wrote the check for payment."

Denni heaved an overly dramatic sigh. "What a guy."

"My hero." Keri's throaty laugh, that laugh of a woman in love and happily fulfilled in marriage, pierced Denni's raw heart. She flinched. As if by design, a tap sounded at the door and Ruth poked her head in. "Oh, good. You're up."

"Who's talking?" Keri asked.

"It's Ruth. I need to go."

"All right. I just wanted to wish you a happy birthday anyway. Have a great one, okay?"

"Sure, Ker. Thanks for calling."

"Hey, wait."

"Yeah?"

"You all right?"

Tears sprang to Denni's eyes. "Yeah. Just the birthday blues."

Ruth cleared her throat. "I made biscuits and gravy," she said in a loud whisper.

Denni nodded and Ruth pulled the door shut, leaving her alone once more.

"Keri. I'm going to slip downstairs for breakfast."

"Okay. But promise you won't be depressed. This is your year for love, sister. I can feel it."

"Who said it has anything to do with love?"

The sound of Keri's chuckle filled her ears just before she disconnected the call.

"A birthday party?" Reece blinked at the rookie sitting next to him on the barstool of Al's café. Today they were wedged together like a can of tennis balls. He hated crowds.

Sean grinned. "Yeah. And Leigh says it won't be the same without you."

"Why? Does she plan on using me for the piñata?"

A guffaw shook Sean and he slapped Reece on the back with enough force to dislodge a hunk of steak, if there had been one caught in his throat. "I wouldn't put it past her. Seriously, though. I think she just wants to make Denni happy and she knows having you show up would do it."

Reece let out a bitter laugh and dunked a fry in a well of ketchup. "Yeah, well. Leigh needs to get some updated information if that's what she thinks."

"What are you saying?"

"Denni called it all off between us. She's more interested in God than she is in me."

Sean's eyes grew wide. "You mean she's going to be a nun or a preacher or something?"

Scowling, Reece tossed a fry backwards. It hit its mark, Sean's nose. "Hey!"

"She isn't going to be a nun. She just doesn't want to date a guy who doesn't think God's very necessary. That's all."

"Wow. Sorry, man." Sean meant it. The tenderhearted rookie cop had been through his own set of heartaches lately. First falling in love with a girl he'd only meant to make fall for *him*—well, that one probably served him right. But having to arrest the woman he loved, in a strip club of all places, had to wrench his guts out.

"So you're still dating Leigh, huh?"

Sean's face clouded. "I figure there's still more to learn. Especially from a girl who keeps such good secrets."

"Uh-huh." Reece wasn't buying it.

"And I guess I'm not ready to stop seeing her." He admitted. "I like her a lot."

Reece cast him a sidelong glance. The misery on the kid's face shot straight to Reece's heart. "Sometimes you just can't help it. Even if you know it's the wrong girl."

Surprise lifted Sean's brow and Reece winced at his own admission. He jammed another fry into his mouth. His association with Denni had turned him into a big wimp. Next he'd be writing poetry and buying sappy cards.

"So when is this party supposed to be?"

"Tonight. It's sort of being thrown together last-minute. I guess the idea came to her stepmom in a dream." He chuckled. "That's one feisty woman."

"I know she is. That's what I like most about her. From her soft looks, you'd never guess she would be."

"Soft looks? Ruth?"

"Ruth?" Reece frowned. "I was talking about Denni."

"Oh, man. You've got it so bad for that one. You might as well go buy a suit."

"Suit?"

"A Sunday-go-to-meetin' suit. And don't forget to say 'amen' real loud every few minutes. That'll get you in real good with the preacher."

Reece shoved up from the barstool. "Let's go."

"I'm not done with my lunch." Sean shoveled in a huge bite of his cheeseburger and chewed hard and fast.

"Yes you are."

"Where are we going now?"

"I have an appointment with the caterer Denni was supposed to use a couple of weeks ago. Her sister is a liaison for one of the churches who might sponsor the Mahoney House project."

"So?"

"The caterer said someone cancelled at the last minute. Only no one did. Denni and I had to scramble to get a lunch together."

Reece's stomach jumped at the memory. That had been a great day.

Sean walked his tray to the trash bin, slurping down the last of his soda. "Funny, I can't picture you in an apron."

"Shut up," Reece growled. He pushed open the door and let it begin to close. Sean caught it easily.

"So what's the crime?"

"You're annoying me, that's what."

"I mean the caterer. Sheesh. Focus, will you?"

Reece felt like popping the kid. But he had to admit he was a little rattled. His all-consuming thoughts about Denni Mahoney distracted him. He was losing the woman he loved. *Loved?* He gulped and thought about it a second. Yep. *Loved.* Real love. Death-do-us-part kind of stuff.

"So, the caterer. Why do you think we need to talk to her?"

All right. Time to focus. Sean was right.

"Like I said, her sister was at the luncheon."

"So?"

"So she let it slip that she knew the luncheon was cancelled and still she showed up—dressed in a business suit and ready to look around."

"I see little dots, but nothing I can really connect. Is there more?"

They slid into the unmarked Crown Vic. Reece cranked the engine and maneuvered into traffic.

"Miss Wilson and Denni have a history that goes back to the time Denni worked for Division of Family Services. Miss Wilson wanted to be a foster parent. Denni had to turn her down."

A low whistle streamed from between Sean's lips. "So she might be holding a grudge. And if she's got problems upstairs in the brain department, that grudge might even be strong enough to make her do things like turn on water faucets and set empty tea kettles on burners."

"Exactly."

"So why are we just now getting around to interviewing the sister?"

"Because she left for vacation the day after the luncheon. I finally got in touch with her this morning and she said to come by after one."

"What a coincidence."

"Yeah, want to know what else is a coincidence?"

"Huh?"

"Elizabeth just pulled out of her sister's parking lot."

Chapter Sixteen

The short, plump blonde was about as much the opposite of Elizabeth Wilson's six-foot Amazon-type figure as you could get.

"So, there's not much resemblance between the two of you," Reece said, keeping his voice deliberately pleasant. Maybe it would be an icebreaker. So far she had pretty much just glared.

"That's because we're not blood sisters."

"Which one was adopted?"

"Both of us. Our mother couldn't have children, so she made a career of adopting unwanted kids."

"Oh." Sean cast him a hmmm-very-interesting look. Reece inwardly winced. He was going to have to talk to the kid about working on his poker face.

Reece gave Linda Wilson what he knew was a winning grin. He wasn't without his charm, and he knew it. Still, guilt wormed through his stomach, accompanied by a healthy dose of frustration. Why did he suddenly feel as though he was cheating on Denni by flirting harmlessly with a potential witness?

But it worked. Linda de-iced a bit, giving him an uncertain smile in return. "What exactly is it that you think I can do for you, detectives?"

"One detective," Reece said, keeping the smile fixed. "He's just an officer."

A blush crept to her cheeks. "Sorry."

"It's all right. But to answer your question. Someone has been causing Miss Mahoney all kinds of trouble. The luncheon wasn't supposed to have been cancelled. And yet it was."

"I feel terrible about that. But the caller had the order number and knew everything on the menu." Her face was still flushed and Reece wondered if her blood pressure was going up.

"I'm sure it was an honest mistake on your part, Linda. But someone was messing with Miss Mahoney's luncheon. Trying to sabotage her efforts to buy a couple of houses just like that one so she can help more girls. It was an important event that she had to pull together at the last second. All by herself."

Sean cleared his throat. "With a little help from her friends."

Reece glared at him, then readjusted his expression and turned back to the plump little cook.

"Anything you can remember about the person's voice or something they might have said that struck you as particularly odd might be helpful."

"I'm sorry, detective. As I said, the person calling had all the information I require to cancel an order on such short notice."

"You didn't recognize the voice?"

"No. But Miss Mahoney had spoken with me only a couple of times during the two months since she booked me to cater her luncheon. I wouldn't have recognized her voice."

That sounded reasonable. He was ninety-nine percent sure that she was telling the truth. "I see. Do you know why she chose your business in particular to cater the luncheon?"

Linda's eyes narrowed. "What difference does that make? And what exactly are you getting at anyway? You know about Elizabeth, so don't you think it's logical to assume she had something to do with a recommendation for me?"

Hmm, a girl who spoke her mind. Got straight to the point.

"Another thing. I checked with the travel agent and discovered that you booked your vacation the night of the luncheon. Are you always so impulsive?"

Her face was definitely red. "No. Not usually. But that cancellation really was the last straw in a series of bad jobs. I only started the business a year ago. It takes awhile to get off the ground. I—I just needed a break."

Reece nodded. "Sounds reasonable. Are you feeling more rested?"

"I was until our little chat."

Reece chuckled. Touché. "There's just one more question and I'll be out of here."

Her face relaxed. "All right."

"Do you know why someone would go to a luncheon they knew had been cancelled?"

Her eyes narrowed with suspicion. "What are you getting at, detective?"

"I think you know."

"If you're implying my sister had anything to do with Miss Mahoney's problems, you are way off base."

"But you did tell your sister that the luncheon was cancelled and yet she went anyway?"

"Yes."

"Do you know why she would do that?"

Linda measured him with her gaze as if deciding how much to tell him. When she spoke, he instinctively felt her sincerity. "She thought Denni had cancelled the luncheon because she wasn't prepared. I mean, no one could have known that I told Elizabeth it was cancelled, so she decided to show up anyway, play dumb, and get an impromptu look at the house."

Linda blushed again. "We're not young women, Detective. It doesn't take much to make us happy. Elizabeth thought she'd get brownie points with the pastor if she scoped out Denni's house and found out whether it was really worthy of receiving another grant or not."

"And what made her think she could really be an impartial judge?" Reece felt his anger rise at the woman who obviously wanted to see Denni fail.

"My sister isn't holding a grudge, if that's what you're implying, Detective. She only wants to be sure the Lord's money isn't misspent."

"I guess you know her better than I do." Reece gathered a deep breath. "There's nothing more for us here." He walked to the door. Then turned. "Oh, I'm sorry. There is just one more thing. Did Elizabeth know we were coming today?"

"I— Well, she…" She shrugged. "Yes, she did."

"And what did she have to say about it?"

Seemingly taken aback by the question, the woman raised her chin and met his gaze head-on. "Only that she hoped no one was accusing her of anything just because Denni Mahoney denied her a chance at motherhood. But don't read anything into it. She's dramatic that way. She didn't mean it like it sounds."

"I hope not. Because it sounds like she might be a woman bent on revenge."

"Trust me. She's not. My sister has had her share of trouble and she doesn't want any more. And if you really want to know why she was here today, I'll tell you."

"All right. Why?" As if he didn't know.

"Apparently my customers have missed me, because I came home to a huge batch of orders and I needed help. My sister came over to bail me out of a bind. It was a coincidence."

Sure it was. With his hand on the door, Reece flashed her another smile. "Thank you for your cooperation, Linda. We appreciate it."

"Detective! Wait."

Reece turned back.

Her face was red again. "I lied to you earlier."

He froze.

"I mean I lied about why I left so suddenly. I've been in a relationship for two years. The day I got the call about the luncheon being cancelled, I also got a call from him, ending things." Tears filled her eyes. "He found someone else."

Reece rubbed his head, anxiety rising. If she was going to cry, he was out of there.

Sean came to the rescue. "I'm sorry. It was his loss."

Linda smiled, "That was really the last straw. And the reason I decided to go on vacation."

And that explained the red face, Reece thought. His gut told him that Linda had shared everything she knew now. Which meant that while Elizabeth might not want Mahoney House to succeed, she hadn't called the caterer to cancel. As he left the house, his suspect list shifted like sand through an hourglass. There was nothing easy about this case.

"Surprise!"

Denni's smile froze as clarity came rushing over her. She was the victim of a surprise party. A sigh rushed to her lips, but she disguised it as a gasp of pleasure before it could escape and give away her true feelings about surprise parties, and birthdays after the age of thirty, in general. There would be no sliding gracefully into any new year closer to old age.

"Look, she's speechless. That's never happened before." Keri's unmistakable voice brought a round of laughter. She stepped up and gave Denni a quick hug, then stepped aside as Raven followed suit. "So, you finally get to be the center of attention." She grinned. "How does it feel?"

Denni gave a short laugh at her beautiful sister's ridiculous question. "You're asking me how it feels to be center of attention? That's a laugh." She hugged Raven. "Thanks for coming," she whispered. "How's the anchor job coming along?"

"Becca's still working her dad so he'll get her firmly placed in that anchor chair."

"Is it working?"

"Of course." Raven grinned. "Too bad the guy's married. I'd go after him and make him fall in love. Then he'd have to give me the job."

"Way to have a plan, Rave." Denni laughed, knowing her sister would no more use her beauty to get a job than she would defile herself with a filet mignon.

Denni glanced around the living room. Ruth beamed

like a woman with a secret just begging to come out. "Ruth," she said, giving the woman a tight squeeze. "This must have been all your idea."

"Yes, ma'am. And everyone jumped on it like a duck on a June bug."

"I appreciate it, everyone."

Only Leigh was noticeably absent, but Denni knew she had to work. Denni continued to peruse the room and her heart nearly stopped at the sight of Reece, leaning against the wall, his thumbs resting jauntily in his belt loops. He sent her a lazy grin and she thought her heart might pound from her chest. Even after she'd broken off any chance of a relationship with him, he'd still come to her birthday party?

She started toward him just as the bell rang, taking her attention. Only a couple of steps from the door, she reached for the doorknob and pulled. Her stomach lurched at the sight of Mrs. James and Sarah standing there. "Were we too loud? We have a lot of people in here."

"No. You weren't too loud."

"Well then…"

"Mrs. James," Ruth's voice, filled with delight, spoke over Denni's shoulder. "You came, after all. We're so glad you did. And look, you brought Sarah with you."

The old lady "harrumphed" and looked highly offended. "She didn't even know I was coming. Looked at me like I didn't belong." Sarah looked ill at ease, her eyes shifting around the room, shoulders slumped.

Ruth swept the old lady and her aging daughter into the room. "Of course Denni didn't know you were coming. She didn't even know *she* was coming. This is a surprise party, remember?"

The old lady's face lit up. "Now I do. Glad I didn't spill the beans."

Denni stepped up. "Thanks so much for coming to my birthday party. It means a great deal to me."

"I was proud to be asked. Especially after you talked that policeman into raising my fence for me so that Buffy doesn't run off anymore." She smiled again and handed Denni a package wrapped in Christmas paper. "That was all I had on such short notice."

Denni laughed, and didn't bother to set the record straight—that Reece and Sean had seen fit to take care of the fence as a favor to her rather than to the elderly widow. "The paper is just perfect. I love Christmas."

An hour later, the party was in full swing. "Happy Birthday" had been sung slightly off pitch, but she had loved every wrong note of it. With a moment to breathe, she flopped onto the couch, slipped off her toe-pinching sandals and smiled at Cate. "How are you feeling?"

Cate gave a weary sigh. "A little tired. I'll be so glad when this baby comes."

"The day will be here before you know it."

A slight frown creased the girl's brow. "Do you think I'm making the right decision?"

"On whether to keep the baby?"

The girl nodded.

Denni sucked in a cool breath. She'd tried not to give her opinion on this subject. The girl was so adamant about not tossing her child aside the "way her mom had."

"I don't know, Cate. It's a tough decision. You have to make the choice that you can live best with."

"How will she feel, though, knowing I just gave her away? If I treat her like she was some kind of mistake?"

Denni scooted over and slipped her arm around

Cate's shoulders. Tears glistened in the mother-to-be's eyes. "How am I going to take care of her, Denni?"

"May I pray with you?"

Cate bobbed her head. And they closed their eyes. Denni prayed for peace and wisdom. She reminded God that Cate only wanted to do the right thing. And asked Him to reveal His plan for the baby and for Cate.

When she opened her eyes, Cate's face seemed more serene. "Thanks, Denni." She squeezed her hand. "I'm going into the kitchen to nab me a slice of that cake. In a few more weeks, I'm going to have to start the diet roller-coaster again. Might as well take advantage of the end-of-pregnancy hunger while I can."

Denni smiled and watched Cate waddle into the kitchen. Sensing attention on her, Denni glanced around, looking for the source. Her breath caught when her gaze rested on Reece. After a cursory happy birthday earlier, he had pretty much left her to mingle with the rest of the "family."

He started to walk toward her, just as a loud knock on the door interrupted their would-be meeting. Reece sent her a lopsided grin and shrugged as she pushed up from the couch and made her way to the door.

Elizabeth Wilson stood on the porch, shaking with fury. Her heels clacked on the porch as she paced.

"Elizabeth?"

"Just what do you think you're trying to prove? Do you honestly think I have nothing better to do than to set fires in *your* house?"

Denni stepped back at the verbal assault. "What are you talking about? Of course you didn't set any fires."

"Then call off your watchdog."

"Dog? When did you folks get a dog?" Mrs. James asked in the tense silence of the room.

Reece stepped forward. "I believe I'm the watchdog Miss Wilson is referring to."

The elderly woman lifted her chin. "That's ridiculous."

"How about if we step out onto the porch and talk about this?" Reece suggested, taking Elizabeth firmly by the arm.

The irate woman jerked free. "I will not stand for this defamation of character." Her lips trembled and Denni's heart melted in compassion. "I have worked too hard to regain my dignity. To—to…"

"Please, Elizabeth," Denni said, stepping between Reece and the distraught woman. "Come and sit down. Reece, please go into the kitchen and get Elizabeth a glass of punch."

"Don't bother," Elizabeth said with a sniff.

"You'll love it, trust me. Ruth made it with scoops of lime sherbet. It's really good."

Elizabeth expelled a heavy sigh. "Fine."

Reece sent Denni a deep scowl that pretty much let her know what he thought of being her errand boy. Denni smiled at him, to let him know she couldn't care less what he thought. If he hadn't been barking up the wrong tree in the first place, Elizabeth wouldn't be sitting on her couch, during her party, most likely getting ready to reject her application for a grant.

Chapter Seventeen

Reece sat on the barstool in Denni's kitchen, his fingers wrapped around a cup of steaming coffee—if it could be called that. His mood was about as foul as the sludge he'd poured from the bottom of the pot.

Since when had he gotten himself so connected to a woman that she could tell him to get lost without uttering a word?

That's exactly what Denni had done. And he felt the sting of it, just remembering. He'd carried two paper cups filled with green globs of sherbet floating in red punch, to Denni and Elizabeth. He'd had every intention of dominating that conversation. Instead, he'd gotten distracted when Denni's fingers had brushed his while the cup was being exchanged from his hand to hers. When her gaze lifted to his, the message was clear: take a hike and stop hounding Elizabeth.

So now he found himself alone, in the deserted kitchen, drinking the bottom of the pot, which was fitting, since he felt like a bottom-dweller himself.

Footsteps on the linoleum alerted him and he looked up. "Hi, Mac."

"Hey, now. What are you doing in here all by yourself? Don't you know there's a party going on in there?"

Reece gave a short laugh. "What are *you* doing in here?"

Mac sent him a sheepish grin. "Parties are for the young. I took on out of there lickety-split before Ruthie could get jealous and accuse me of flirting with that cute little curly-headed girl."

Real amusement now filled Reece, lifting his spirits. It figures Mac would think Rissa and her fake Southern-belle accent were cute.

Mac walked over to the coffeepot, stared at the empty decanter and sighed.

"Sorry, I got the last of it." Reece help up his mug for emphasis. "You're not missing much, believe me."

"Ah, just as well."

"What are you doing, Dad?"

Raven breezed in, her eyes narrowing as she looked from Mac to the empty coffeepot.

"Nothing. There's not a drop left for me to take."

"Good. You don't need the caffeine with that blood pressure of yours." She walked over and planted a kiss on his cheek. "I'll find some decaf and make a nice fresh pot of non-blood-pressure-raising coffee."

Mac patted her cheek and took a seat on another stool. "Aren't my daughters the best?"

"Sure they are," Reece said, thinking of one daughter in particular. Denni was the best for him. That was one reality he couldn't escape.

He sipped at the bitter-tasting liquid.

"So, Reece. Denni says you've been on this case for

awhile now. Why do you think you've been unsuccessful in finding the person responsible for Denni's troubles?"

Denni's sister had that hard-nosed-reporter face on. The one he'd seen a thousand times from the local press. And he wasn't impressed. Especially when she seemed to be implying that he wasn't doing his job.

"I'd say a lot of that has to do with Denni's insistence that no one could possibly be behind it."

"No one?" Raven pushed the button and a red light came on just as the pot began to brew.

"Apparently, there must be a phantom here out to cause all this mischief, because your sister won't admit that even one person she knows could possibly be out to do her harm."

"Well, that's just Denni. She's like a mother who staunchly believes in her kids." Raven leaned on her elbows. "You'll just have to stop trying to get a date and do your job."

Anger bit him hard and he frowned. This girl was definitely looking for a fight.

Mac chuckled. "That's my daughter. Straight to the point. But I have to agree with her. You are too worried about getting close to my Denni. Find whoever is doing these things, and save the romancing until afterwards."

"Yeah," Raven gave him a quirky little grin. "A girl can't resist a hero."

"She can if he doesn't go to church."

A groan sounded from Raven's throat and she rolled her eyes. "You're kidding? She's keeping you at bay because of church?"

She made a good point as far as Reece was concerned.

"Raven, honey," Mac broke in, "You know the way things work." He turned to Reece. "You two might be happy in the beginning, but eventually, the relationship would turn sour. You'd want things from her she couldn't give you. And you'd resent it."

Reece's cheeks blazed. "I'd marry her." *What??* He most certainly would *not!*

"That's noble of you," Mac replied. "But Denni was raised to know that God has to be first. His ways are higher than ours even if we don't understand them, or particularly like them. And He does have His reasons."

Raven snorted. "When two people are right for each other, they should be together. Regardless of any so-called rules."

"Well, that's your opinion, missy," Mac growled.

Reece was tempted to tell him to watch his blood pressure. Raven poured a cup of the decaf that had just finished brewing. She set it on the counter in front of Mac and laid her head on his shoulder. "I'm sorry, Dad. Denni has to do what she thinks is right." She looked up and winked at Reece. "But if she isn't careful, some other girl without the same standards is going to come along and snatch the handsome detective right out from under her nose."

Reece returned her wink and shook his head. Not a chance of that ever happening. Denni was his one and only and if he couldn't have her...well, he'd managed to stay single for thirty-five years. The next fifty years or so shouldn't be that much of a problem.

"Hey, you three are missing all the fun." Keri breezed into the room and grabbed a cup of punch from the table. "Justin and the boys just put on the Macarena."

"Is that song *ever* going to go away?" Raven asked, not even bothering to hide her smirk.

"Nope. It's become pop culture. It's here to stay, along with the Hokey Pokey and the Chicken Dance."

"Ugh. Let's don't start talking about the Chicken Dance. I'll never forget the humiliation of doing it at high-school basketball games."

"Ahh, the price of being a perky little cheerleader," Keri said with a laugh. "I think Denni's about ready to open gifts. You coming?"

"Yep." Raven pressed a kiss to Mac's balding head. "Let's go."

Reece followed. He thought of his gift out in the truck but decided to wait. Maybe he'd give it to her later. A grin played at the corners of his lips. He didn't want to share her attention when she saw his gift.

Denni smiled and thanked each person for their gift. From Ruth and Dad she'd been given a sizable check to go toward Mahoney House. With all the repairs lately, it would definitely come in handy. The electric bill, for one thing, came to mind.

The girls had chipped in and got her a gift certificate to a local day spa. Raven had bought her a full-length leather jacket she'd been dying for, but never would have spent the money on in a hundred years. Keri, Justin and the boys had bought her a complete set of C. S. Lewis's *Chronicles of Narnia*. Hardback and leatherbound. Secretly, this was the gift Denni most treasured. And Mrs. James had brought her a plaque with a line from "Mending Wall" by Robert Frost, Good Fences Make Good Neighbors etched into the wood.

Denni had to choke back a laugh at the sentiment. It should have read Taller Fences Make Good Neighbors. Things had been much calmer since Reece and Sean had raised that fence. After several more minutes, the gift-opening came to a conclusion and everyone went back to mingling.

Raven grabbed her hand. "I don't know about you, but I'm ready for cake and ice cream."

"Oooh, me too. Let's go."

"Everyone, let's rally. The birthday girl wants her cake," Raven called, commanding attention.

"Does she want to eat it too?" Rissa's overblown Southern accent rose above the crowd, her corny joke inciting a wave of laughter.

"Yeah, I do, so I want to hear some singing."

"Wait, we have to light the candles." Ruth's voice rose in panic. She shot across the room faster than Denni would have thought possible for a woman her age. Her eyes shot Denni a warning. "Don't come near this kitchen until I have the cake prepared. You hear?"

"I hear." Denni smiled.

"Sounds like it might be a good time for my gift." Reece's voice next to her ear, sent a shiver through Denni.

"You cold?" he asked.

Nervous laughter bubbled from Denni. "In this stuffy room? I don't think so."

"My gift is in the truck. Will you come outside with me?"

"You shouldn't have gotten me a gift, Reece."

"Only a creep goes to a birthday party without a gift."

"You could never be a creep." The words left her before she thought.

Reece's eyes grew dark with emotion. He slipped his arm around her, resting his palm against the small of her back. "Come on."

Warmth spread out from his fingers, across her back

and Denni could no more have refused his simple request than she could have woven gold from her hair.

Once outside, in the glow of the porch light, Reece waved her toward the swing. "I'll be right back."

Denni exhaled a breath as she sat in the coolness of the summer night. A gentle breeze sang through the leaves and she could have sworn a love song was being composed on her behalf.

"Here you go."

She smiled at Reece and took the gift he held out. He dropped into the swing next to her. Denni could feel his tension as she slowly removed the gorgeous purple ribbon and tore into the paper. A soft gasp escaped her and quick tears sprang to her eyes. "Oh, Reece." In a beautiful cherrywood frame was an eight-by-ten photograph of Denni and her mother. One that had nearly been destroyed in the flooded basement. Lovingly, she fingered the edges of the picture frame.

"You like it?" he whispered.

"How can you even ask?" She stared at him. "How did you do this?"

"I sent it away to a shop in Kansas City that restores old photos. I just happened to get it back last week and knew it would make a perfect birthday gift."

"It does," she said. "It's the most perfect gift I've ever received." Without even considering the implications, she moved close and wrapped her arms around his neck, she pressed her mouth close to his ear. "Thank you, Reece. From the bottom of my heart."

She felt his quick intake of breath and his fingers pressed against her back. She pulled away, inches from his face. He squinted and fixed her with his gaze, searching.

Denni smiled and pressed a quick kiss to his cheek,

then slipped out of his grasp before he could take it further. Nothing had changed. Not her feelings, and not the aching reality that he didn't share her faith.

The door opened and Keri poked her head out. "All right, birthday girl, the candles are all lit. Get in here before someone calls the fire department."

"Denni is mocking you." Mother's voice hissed in her ear. And the old hag knew she couldn't say anything back. The whole room would hear. She glared at Mother, but that didn't shut her up. "Look at her. She's having a good time, isn't she?"

Denni was smiling, especially at the detective.

Anger burned.

"Do you think Denni deserves to have a good time?"

No, no she didn't deserve it. Not at all.

"When? When will you make her pay?"

"Patience, Mother," she whispered, then glanced about to be sure no one had heard her.

A ring of laughter rose up from the crowd in the room. She must have missed the joke. Now everyone was filing out of the room toward the kitchen. Everyone but Denni. Denni was headed her way.

She gritted her teeth as Denni walked by and winked, as though everything were fine between them. As though they were best friends. What kind of reality did Denni Mahoney live in?

"What are you doing all by yourself in a corner? Go mingle." Denni grinned. She had never seen Denni so happy. But all that was about to change.

"Ask her where she's going," Mother commanded in her ear.

"Where are you going, Denni?"

"Down to the laundry room to get a case of pop from the shelf. This is one thirsty bunch."

Silent glee flowed through her. Her opportunity. She'd waited like a trooper through the opening of the gifts, the blowing out of the candles. And now, her patience was about to pay off. Because Denni was going down to the basement. And basements were the perfect places to get rid of unwanted things. And people. And this was it. She'd waited long enough.

Watching Denni leave the room, her heart began to pound. Finally. Finally, Denni was going to get what she deserved.

She started to follow her.

"Wait!"

"What, Mother?"

"You can't just follow her. What if someone is watching?"

That was true. She'd detour through the kitchen.

Her palms dampened in anticipation and she slowly made her way toward the kitchen. Only Ruth stood in the room, her hands plunged into a sinkful of sudsy water.

This was getting better and better.

"Where is everyone?" Mother asked.

"Where is everyone?" she repeated to Ruth.

"Oh, hi, sweetie. You know they all had to go out and take a look at the new fence."

"I see. Maybe I'll join them."

"You do that, honey."

With a cautious glance around, she slipped toward the basement. No one was in sight as she slowly opened the basement door and closed it behind her. Her hand touched the light switch on the wall at the top of the stairs and pressed it down. Darkness overwhelmed the room. She pulled her flashlight from her waistband and switched it on. Slowly she descended the stairs.

A shadow that could only be Denni, poked her head out of the laundry room at the bottom of the stairs. She squinted against the light shining in her eyes. "Who is it? Wh-what are you doing?"

Oh, no. She wasn't about to speak and give herself away. Before Denni could react, she snatched the crescent wrench from the table next to the laundry-room door. She knew what she had to do. Her arm came up, just as Denni's eyes went wide with horror.

Chapter Eighteen

A scream tore at Denni's throat, but no sound escaped. The sickening thud of something smashing against her skull exploded in her head, along with pain such as she'd never known.

The ground rose up to meet her. Blackness invaded her world. As if in a dream, she felt fingers wrap around her ankles and pull her...*where?* Her body wouldn't obey her commands. *Fight. Scream. Fight. Scream. Dear God, why can't I move? Am I dying?*

She heard footsteps, then someone stepped over her. A door closed... Then she smelled gas. Tears filled her eyes. She was going to die. And she'd never told Reece she loved him. She would never know the joy of watching him surrender his heart to Jesus.

Send someone to him, Lord. Please let me see him in Heaven some day.

General consensus was that the addition to the fence looked a little odd, but that it worked and that was what mattered most. Reece accepted the praise and the criticism and figured as long as Buffy stayed in her own back yard he had successfully met his objective.

Reece smelled the gas as soon as he came inside the house. He glanced at Ruth, who was wiping up the counter.

"Where's the gas smell coming from, Ruth?"

"What do you mean? I don't smell any... Oh, yes I do. Mercy! I didn't even notice."

He turned and blocked the entrance. "Stay outside. Gas is leaking from somewhere. I'm going to check it out." He glanced at Ruth. "You join Mac and the others outside, all right?"

"Where's Denni?"

"I don't know. Last I saw her she was headed down to the basement to get another case of pop. But come to think of it, she should have been back by now."

How long did it take to get a case of soda? Reece headed toward the basement steps. The smell of gas stung his nose, becoming stronger the closer he got to the basement. When he opened the door, it was almost overwhelming.

Without looking back, he plunged into the darkness of the basement. "Denni!"

"Reece?" Raven called from upstairs, shining a flashlight down the stairs. "What's going on? I smell gas."

"Bring me that flashlight."

An instant later she handed it to him.

"Where's the light switch?" Reece called.

"Right here, I got it."

Immediately the darkness fled. He looked around. There was no sign of Denni. "Denni!"

No answer.

Raven joined him. "Here. The door to the laundry

room is locked from the inside." She pounded on the door. "Denni! Denn! Open up!"

"Move out of the way," Reece ordered. He raised his foot high and kicked with as much force as he possessed. The door smashed open.

Oh, God, please let her be okay, he prayed at the sight of the woman he loved laid out facedown on the cold concrete.

Raven covered her mouth as a cough rose from within her chest. "That smell is bad. I'm feeling a little disoriented. We have to get her out of here now. She's already been down here long enough that it's dangerous."

Reece knelt and gathered Denni in his arms. "I'll get you out of here, sweetheart." He cradled her head in his hand as he carried her up the steps. He was mildly aware that his palm had become sticky with what could only be fresh blood. This was no accident. Whoever did this hadn't meant for Denni to leave that laundry room alive.

Please, please God. Don't let her die.

Denni heard the sound of her own moan as she slowly approached consciousness. Panic lit a fire in her stomach. Something was over her face! Were they trying to suffocate her?

"It's all right, Denn." The sound of Raven's voice sent a wave of relief over her. "It's only an oxygen mask on your face. You're being treated for carbon monoxide poisoning. Somebody up there must think you're pretty special, because if you had been in that room five more minutes, you'd most likely be dead or brain-damaged at the very least."

Denni nodded. She remembered praying at the very

end. Praying for Reece. *Thank you for sparing my life, Lord.*

From the corner of her eye, she saw the door open. Raven looked toward the creaking.

"Is she awake?"

Denni's heart jumped at the sound of Reece's voice.

Raven glanced back down, squeezed her hand, and winked. "Someone down here thinks you're pretty special too. He kicked down the door and carried you out of that room." She gave her a broad wink. "Sounds like a man in love. Know what I mean?"

Denni gave a weary nod. She was too tired to argue. In a flash, Raven moved away and Reece stood over her. He covered her hand, his warmth chasing away the cold from her fingers. "The doctor says you're going to be all right."

"Thanks to you," she said, her voice muffled through the mask.

He nodded, acknowledging the truth of what he'd done, but the tenderness in his eyes held no pride or ego. Just a calm acceptance. "Can you remember who hit you?"

Denni closed her eyes and shook her head, trying to focus. All she remembered was a woman's form. Something coming toward her head, falling, being dragged by her ankles. Her shirt had hiked up and the concrete on her stomach had been uncomfortably cold.

She opened her eyes and looked into his. The gentle concern reflected in his gaze melted her heart. Reece was such a good man. If only He could accept God's love for him...

"Sorry. I can't remember any more, and I didn't get a look at the person anyway." Frustrated, she pulled the mask from her face. "I can't talk with this thing on."

Reece slowly moved her hand away and replaced the mask. "Then we'll wait until you can talk. Don't take that off until the doctor gives you the all-clear. Understand?"

His gentle reprimand felt more like a request and Denni couldn't refuse. She nodded.

"Just let me talk," Reece said softly.

He raised her hand to his lips and gently pressed a kiss to her knuckles. Then he lifted her hand to his cheek until she could feel the warm scratchy growth beneath her palm.

"Reece," she whispered into the mask.

He brushed the top of her nose with his index finger. "No talking," he said. "We had a deal. I want to tell you something."

Denni nodded.

"I know that you can't be with me unless I believe in God like you do." He beamed at her. "Well, I'm going to go to church with you."

Oh, Reece. That's not it. Her heart cried out. *God, show him that it's not about pleasing me or going to church. It's about knowing You.*

She relaxed with his next words. "I can't promise to understand everything the preacher says or even agree with what I do understand. If a woman with your intelligence believes so strongly in God, there must be something to it."

Denni danced on the inside. Reece was coming around. God was drawing him. It wouldn't be long now until he made that decision about Jesus. The decision that would change his life forever.

Apparently oblivious to her line of thinking, Reece continued. "The—um the doctor said it's amazing you made it. The gas line was cut and you were lying right in front of it. If you hadn't somehow turned your face away, you'd be dead. As it is, the doctor is shocked that you're doing as well as you are. The levels of gas were high, but not anywhere near the highest levels. Only God could have saved you."

Denni's heart thrilled at the admission coming from his lips.

The door opened again and Ruth and Mac bustled into the room. Reece released Denni's hand and stepped back. She followed his movement with her eyes. With a wink and a smile, he promised her that everything would be all right.

Reece leaned against the wall watching Mac and Ruth fuss over Denni. The nurse had told them only two visitors allowed at a time, but being a cop had its advantages. The petite little brunette, who couldn't have been more than a year or two out of nursing school, reluctantly agreed that he could stay, as long as he promised not to interfere with the patient's treatment.

Denni motioned to Ruth, making the gesture of a person writing. "Paper? You want a pen and paper?" The volume of Ruth's voice rose as though Denni were deaf. Reece chuckled.

Ruth rummaged through her purse and produced the items Denni had requested.

Mac interpreted. "Are the girls okay?"

"Yeah. Everyone in the house was given a blood test, but you're the only one who needed treatment."

"Where is everyone staying tonight?"

"Oh, I sprang for a few rooms at the Holiday Inn. Keri's boys are having fun playing in the swimming pool."

Relief flooded Denni's face. Then she gave the tiniest hint of a sad smile and began to write again. "Did I miss God's will for my life?"

"What do you mean, honey?" Ruth asked.

"Was this all an ego thing? My way of making myself feel better about mom dying when I was just about the same age as these girls? What if my motives for opening Mahoney House were all wrong?"

Mac took his daughter's hand. "Only God knows what is in a person's heart. The heart has the ability to deceive us."

Denni scrawled again. "So I could be wrong about this being my purpose."

"Everyone was and is made for a reason. God had a plan in mind for you while you were still in your mother's womb. Remember, there are no accidents. The Bible says so. Finding that purpose is always the tricky thing. But honey. Just because there's a struggle doesn't mean God isn't in control."

"And just look," Ruth said, casting a smile at Reece. "He sent you a protector and a friend. Just imagine where you would be through all these bad incidents if this man hadn't been there for you."

A jolt shot through Reece. And a seed of wonder took root. He'd have to ask Mac to show him the verse in the Bible. Was it true that he wasn't an accident? Even if his parents thought he was... God had fooled them and created him for a good reason. He stood a little taller. Maybe his purpose was to look out for Denni. Frankly, Reece couldn't think of a better calling.

Denni felt like shouting for joy when the doctor pronounced her oxygen levels stable enough for her to leave the hospital. After a full twenty-four hours lying abed, she was ready to hit the road. Reece and Cate were waiting for her, so, once she'd dressed, she went in search of the pair. She saw them bent over a book in the waiting room. "What's going on, you two?"

Cate glanced up, and her red-rimmed eyes filled Denni with alarm. "Hey, are you okay? It's not the baby is it?"

She shook her head. "No. It's something Reece just showed me. In the Bible."

"The Bible?" Denni blinked in surprise.

"Yeah," Reece said. "It was just sitting here on the table. Think I shouldn't have picked it up?"

Denni laughed. "No. I think they probably wish a lot more people would pick it up." Curiosity nipped her. "What are you so intent on?"

"Read it to her, please, Reece?" Cate glanced up to meet Denni's gaze. "It's beautiful, Denni."

Reece cleared his throat and glanced uncertainly at Denni. "Go ahead," she urged.

"Well, it says…You made all the delicate, inner parts of my body and knit me together in my mother's womb. Thank you for making me so wonderfully complex. Your workmanship is marvelous—and how well I know it. You watched me as I was being formed in utter seclusion, as I was woven together in the dark of the womb. You saw me before I was born. Every day of my life was recorded in your book. Every moment was laid out before a single day had passed."

He stopped reading and swallowed hard, emotion flickering over his features. "She—uh…" he said jerking a thumb toward Cate, who had teared up once more.

He passed the girl a tissue. "She just needed a little pep talk."

Cate wiped her nose and looked at Denni. "Being at the hospital and having all the nurses think I'm here because I'm in labor just made it more real to me that in a few days, I'm going to be having this baby."

"That's true." Denni smiled her encouragement.

"Reece was the only one around, and I just started talking and crying." She giggled. "Poor guy."

He gave her a lopsided grin that went straight to Denni's heart. "It's all right," he said. "I can take it."

"Anyway," Cate said. "When I said this baby was an accident, Reece said there were no accidents. And when I told him to prove it, he did."

"I'm impressed," Denni said. "That's a favorite scripture of my dad's."

"I know. He told me."

She lifted her brow and stared at Reece. "Dad's been reading the Bible to you?"

He chuckled and shook his head. "I heard him talking to you and asked him where I could find the verse in the Bible. It's just a coincidence that Cate had a relevant concern and I happen to know the Bible verse to make her feel better."

Cate shifted in her seat then gave Denni a teary-eyed gaze. "I think I've finally made a decision, Denni."

"Oh?"

"If God truly made my baby for a purpose, then I can't stand in the way of what she's supposed to be. I've been holding on so that she wouldn't feel like her mama abandoned her. But that was more for me than for her. I—I think God will make sure that she knows how special she is. She'll know that I let her go so that she could live out the story her life is supposed to tell. Like it said in the Bible. I just…I know I can't take care of her."

Tears streamed down the girl's face as she solidified her decision. Denni opened her arms and embraced Cate. "I think you've made a wise and painful choice, Cate. I'm so proud of you."

"Will you help me find an adoption agency?"

"We can do it through the DFS."

Cate shook her head. "I want to go through a private Christian agency. And maybe help pick out the parents. They have to know about this verse. I want my daughter always to know that God writes every page of her life before it even happens."

Denni nodded. "All right. I know of one right here in Rolla. We can call them first thing in the morning."

"Oh, Miss Mahoney," a breathless voice reached her and she turned. "We were afraid you'd gone without signing these forms. And we really do need to wheel you out. Hospital policy."

After completing her release routine, a nurse wheeled Denni outside behind Reece and Cate.

"I hope you don't mind that I picked you up instead of your dad," Reece said, grabbing her hand and lacing his fingers in hers.

Denni thrilled at the contact. She smiled. "Of course not."

Keri and her family had gone back home after assuring themselves that Denni was fine. But Dad and Ruth were still in town. And Raven had called in some personal time in order to do a story on the Mahoney House.

Denni knew what the extra time off meant for her go-getter sister. Each day away from the station, she risked having her dream job slip through her fingers and straight into the lap of a conniving, manipulating new graduate who by all rights should be fetching Raven's coffee.

"I'm a little surprised Dad didn't insist on picking me up, though."

"Let's just say, in the battle of wills, I was the victor."

Cate let out a laugh. "They were in a dead heat until Ruth swung the advantage in Reece's favor by telling Mac you'd rather have Reece come get you. And I rode along because I had a doctor's appointment."

Denni swept over the first part of the comment and focused on the latter. "Oh, what did the doctor say?"

"It could be any time or two weeks."

Denni laughed. "Well, that's why he gets paid the big bucks."

Cate moved ahead, opened the passenger door, and carefully maneuvered her swollen body up into the vehicle.

Reece pulled Denni over to his side and opened the door. "You can sit next to me."

Denni felt heat rush to her cheeks and could find no words. "Are you taking me home?"

He nodded. "The gas company gave it the okay, replaced the hose and installed carbon monoxide detectors."

"Oh, good."

"Your dad and Ruth are at the house cleaning up the party stuff."

Denni's stomach jumped with nerves as they approached her home. For the first time, she wasn't confident about going inside. She loved this house. It had been a gift from God. The amount the previous owners were willing to come down in price and the fact that it was the perfect place to house a group of girls could only be a testimony of God's provision. But now all she could think of was the fact that someone had tried to kill her in her own home.

Would she ever feel safe again?

Chapter Nineteen

Reece rolled his eyes toward the ceiling and sank into his recliner in one motion, toeing off his black dress shoes and kicking up the footrest.

What an exhausting week!

After Denni's close call and overnight hospital stay, he'd spent a solid forty-eight hours on duty, frantically trying to piece together this puzzle of disjointed incidents. It was one thing when there was only theft and sabotage, but now they were investigating an attempted homicide. He hadn't slept in two nights, hadn't eaten in over twenty-four hours, and had sucked down enough coffee to fill a coffee shop. And his body was letting him know just how much it resented the abuse. He was definitely getting too old for this.

With a gnawing sense of dread at confronting the inevitable, he snatched up his phone and dialed his voice mail.

If not for the chance of getting a message from Denni, he would have saved the task until later, but just the thought that he might hear the sound of her sweet voice yanked him from his tendency to procrastinate.

The recorded voice mocked him with the reality of his neglect. Twenty-five—how could he possibly have that many voice messages waiting to be dealt with? He didn't even have that many friends.

Reece growled at the phone, but pushed the chair back to a full recline and settled in to listen to a week's worth of missed calls while he rested his aching back.

Absently, he grabbed the TV remote, pointed it at his dusty TV, and pressed it on.

"Mr. Corrigan," a wimpy male voice on the other end of the phone line said, "This call is to inform you of Jonathon Griggs's demise…"

The voice was shut out by the blast of volume coming from the TV. Reece frantically pressed the volume-down button and the sit-com laughter faded.

"Please contact Mr. Cheney at the Booneville Correctional Center at your earliest convenience."

Reece's heart pounded against his chest as memories slammed to the surface of his mind. Wild images of blood and death and an eighteen-year-old boy high as a kite, standing over the bodies of the dearest people who ever walked the face of the earth.

Nothing short of death or chains would have kept Reece from Jonathon's trial. The prosecution hadn't had to ask or instruct him to testify. He was a more-than-willing participant.

He'd watched Jonathon's expressionless face, every minute of every day during the two-week trial. The jury came back with a guilty verdict within three hours. First-degree murder. Reece had been livid at the verdict of fifty years to life for Jonathon, instead of the death penalty.

He stared at the phone in his hand. It was about time justice was served. Even if Jonathon's death were merely a case of *poetic* justice.

He listened to the message again. "This call is to inform you of Jonathon Griggs's demise. Unfortunately, he passed away of a brain aneurysm at five o'clock yesterday afternoon. I'm sure this is difficult, given the nature of your relationship to Mr. Griggs and the crime for which he was convicted. However, you are listed as next of kin so we have no choice but to contact you. The body has been sent to the city morgue. Unless we hear from you by tomorrow morning, May fifteenth, Mr. Griggs will be cremated and his ashes disposed of. You should also be aware that there are a few personal items that are rightfully yours as next of kin and without a beneficiary specified by Mr. Griggs. Please contact Mr. Cheney at the Booneville Correctional Center at your earliest convenience."

All the energy sifted from Reece as he thumbed off the phone. He had no intention of calling the prison. Today was May seventeenth, so he didn't even have to deal with whether or not to make arrangements to bury the man who had murdered the people who were, for all intents and purposes, Reece's parents. By now, Jonathon was nothing more than a pile of ashes scattered in the wind.

Why would Jonathon have him listed as next of kin, anyway? They were nothing to each other. They had lived as foster brothers for barely a year. Had run with different crowds and essentially didn't get along.

With a shuddering sigh, Reece closed his eyes, trying to squeeze the screaming voice of accusation from his head. The one that said he was as much to blame as Jonathon for his foster parents' death.

* * *

With her elbows resting on the kitchen table, Denni pressed her chin firmly into her palm and blew out a dejected sigh. Over three days. And no word from Reece.

Okay so he had worked solid for two of those days. It wasn't unreasonable that he would need to go home and sleep, shower, do a little laundry maybe. That shouldn't have taken more than twenty-four hours. But it had been a good—she glanced at her watch—thirty-three and a half hours since his shift ended, and still she hadn't heard a peep from him. If the girls hadn't been called in one-by-one for questioning, during his time on duty, she would have thought he'd fallen off the face of the earth.

She'd probably lost a good five pounds just from the calorie-burn of running for the telephone every time it rang.

"Will you focus, already?" Raven pulled her sleek black hair away from her neck and lifted the heavy mound to the top of her head, securing it only with her hand while she glowered at Denni. "I have to leave in just a couple of hours if I'm going to get home in time to avoid rush-hour traffic. Do you want me to do this story or not?"

"I do. You know I do. But I'm having a little trouble concentrating."

"Well, snap out of it. So what if he didn't call for three days? You're the one who told him to get lost."

Denni tossed a towel at her sister's head. "I did not. I just told him I couldn't become involved with him romantically. That didn't mean we couldn't be friends."

Oh, brother. Who was she kidding?

Raven rolled her eyes. "Do you know what that little let's-be-friends speech does to a guy's ego?"

"If anyone knows about that, it's you." Fatigue, loneliness and a general feeling of uneasiness dulled Denni's sensitive nature, and she blurted out her opinion before she could even consider the possibility that Raven might not take it as a joke.

Raven dropped her heavy tresses, which cascaded down her back like a waterfall. "I'm going home." She jumped to her feet and started loading the camera into her bag. "I have enough footage to do a bleeding-heart piece. Janie can edit it and plug in my voice-overs later."

Denni laced her fingers together on the table in front of her. "I'm sorry, Rave. I didn't mean to hurt your feelings."

Raven waved away the apology. "Look, I know you and Keri get a real kick out of my track record with guys. But you know what? I don't want a permanent Mr. Mahoney. And if I did, I'd get one. I like my career. I like dating—no strings attached. And I'm always up front about that. If some egomaniac doesn't believe me and decides he's in love, well, then, I have no choice but to resort to the let's-be-friends speech." She zipped the bag and rested her hands on the black leather. "But you, kiddo, are not me. You adore this man. And Reece is in love with you. You should have seen him carrying you out of that house. If a man ever loved me that way…it might convince me to change my entire philosophy of life in general."

Stunned speechless by Raven's discourse, Denni stared while she processed the monologue. The girls had relived those moments with her countless times, amid sighs and giggles, over the past few days, and Denni thrilled to each telling of it. Too bad she couldn't remember a single second of the most romantic moment of her life. But hearing it through Raven's lips made it more…real. More grown up.

Reece's rescue had been like something out of a romance novel. He was officially her hero, but was he a man in love?

With a scowl, she jammed her chin once more into her palm and stared glumly at her sister. By ignoring her for days, he wasn't acting much like a man in love.

Why was he here? Why the compulsion to contact the prison and get himself roped into the three-hour trip? And what exactly had he said that had induced them to sic the chaplain on him, then make him wait thirty minutes? He glanced about the less-than-homey waiting room and his remaining shred of patience snapped. He ought to just leave. Seriously. That's what he was going to do.

Reece stood, accidentally kicking back the brown, metal chair. The clang resonated off the white concrete walls. Reece winced, feeling as if he'd broken a rule. He bent to pick the chair up just as the door opened.

A middle-aged man, roughly the height of an average-size teenage boy, walked toward him with a confident stride and an outstretched hand. "You must be Detective Corrigan."

Something in his eyes relaxed Reece. Kindness, sympathy, warmth. A sudden and inexplicable longing shot through Reece as he looked into that gentle face and tried to decipher exactly who the guy was feeling sorry for.

Me?

That was laughable. This was the best day of his life. The day he could finally put all thoughts of Jonathon out of his head for good. That's why he'd come. Closure. Once and for all. No more of Jonathon's wild-eyed stare invading his dreams. It was done.

"That for me, Chaplain?" Reece indicated the manila envelope stuffed under the preacher's arm.

"Oh, yeah. Here you go."

With a pounding heart, Reece accepted Jonathon's worldly goods. He fumbled with the fasteners, but hesitated short of examining the contents.

"Do you want me to leave?" the chaplain asked.

Reece felt a little guilty that he'd all but ignored the man since he'd walked into the room. "No. You might as well stick around. As soon as I look at it, I'm out of here, and you can do with his things as you see fit."

"You don't intend to keep any of it?"

Reece listened absently as he tipped the envelope and let the contents fall to the table with a thud and clatter. "No. Why would I?"

"I don't know. I just thought…"

"What?"

"You might find a way to forgive him for what he did if you look through his things—get to know the man he became."

Bewilderment swam over Reece. "What do you mean, forgive him? Why would I want to do that? Besides, he's dead now. So even if I wanted to—which I don't, how would I?"

He smiled. "I don't have any proof, but I'm firmly convinced that forgiveness does more for us than it does for the person we forgive."

"Well, Rev, I appreciate your insight, but I don't happen to want to forgive Jonathon. As a matter of fact, I'm glad he's finally stopped living off the taxpayer's money. Personally, I think he ought to have been chaired to begin with."

"Chaired?"

"Yeah, as in electric."

Understanding dawned in the man's eyes, and Reece could see he was struggling not to show his dismay at Reece's callous answer.

Reece stared at the contents on the table. Letters. Who was writing Jonathon letters, if he'd had no one outside of the prison walls? He picked up an envelope and turned it over. Scrawled on the front was his name. Reece frowned, then he remembered. Three years after Jonathon's incarceration, the letters had started arriving. Like clockwork, once a week. And for five years, Reece had returned every one of them unopened. These must represent a sampling of those. Of the dozen or so envelopes, each carried his name.

He dismissed the letters and glanced at the other items. A decent watch that, ironically, had been a gift from the Ides on Jonathon's eighteenth birthday, shortly before he'd killed them.

Rage snarled up Reece's spine. His fist curled around the watch and in a heartbeat, he pitched it against the wall. The crystal shattered. The chaplain jumped. A guard appeared, his hand resting on the PR-24 hanging from his hip. Reece's senses alerted and he assumed a defensive stance. Cop or no cop, he wouldn't be on the receiving end of that stick.

The chaplain turned and raised his hand. "It's all right."

With a wary glance at Reece the officer stepped reluctantly from the room, leaving the door ajar. The chaplain smiled indulgently and crossed the room. He pushed the door shut then turned back to Reece.

"May I tell you about Jonathon's last years?"

"No."

"All right. How about telling me about yours?"

Resentment welled up in Reece at this preacher's blatant attempt to draw him out. Why was he even staying? He was no prisoner. He could walk through the gates any time he wanted. So what kept him planted to his seat? He glanced at the chaplain.

Those eyes. They weren't effeminate or in any way expressions of weakness. Merely kind. Compelled, and yet uncomfortable at the same time, Reece shifted his gaze back to the items on the table. For the first time he noticed the black book. Like a moth to a flame he couldn't help himself. He reached forward and took the Bible.

A short laugh left him. "Let me guess…Jonathon found the straight and narrow in here?"

"Does that surprise you?"

"Surprise? No." Didn't they all find religion in prison? Wasn't that their way of making it through? No better endorsement than a chaplain's at a parole hearing. "I guess it's pretty typical."

"Jonathon wasn't typical."

The image of those wild eyes flitted across Reece's mind. "No I suppose not." Absently, he flipped open the Bible. His eyebrows lifted. The pages were thin and marked up. Obviously, Jonathon had been trying to make a convincing impression.

"Ironic."

"What?"

"That you'd open to Jonathon's favorite Bible verse."

Reece's first instinct was to smash the book closed, but he couldn't. That shouldn't have surprised him. The entire day had been unreal. He'd gone against every instinct. Just being here in the first place went against every sense of logic he held to. He found himself glancing down at a passage, underlined in red and with stars marking either side of the column.

A wave of dizziness swept him. How could Jonathon have loved *that* verse?

"Jonathon knew that if He could find him in the darkness of prison, then He must also have known him in the darkness of his mother's womb. When he felt alone, it comforted him to know that God was still writing the story of his life."

"I have to go." Reece shoved to his feet and stumbled to the door.

"Wait, detective." The chaplain reached him in a few short strides. He handed Reece the Bible. A few letters were stuffed inside. "At least take this with you."

Reece hesitated, but nodded and grabbed the Bible. He walked through the gates, wishing he'd never come in the first place.

Chapter Twenty

Denni glanced at the clock on the kitchen wall. Forty-eight hours had officially passed since Reece had gotten off duty. Still, not one word. This wasn't like him. Particularly now that he had something concrete to investigate.

So much for Raven's theory about him being a man in love. As a matter of fact, Denni was more than certain that he never had been. And now that he'd saved her life, he was probably worried she'd cling to him like a spider monkey.

Righteous indignation slithered through her at the thought. What was she doing? Sitting around the house like a whiny, waiting, desperate female? She raised her chin in silent defiance of her own folly.

No more waiting. She, Denni Mahoney, was ready to get on with her life. Reece Corrigan or no Reece Corrigan.

When a knock sounded at her door, she jumped, nearly tipping her mug of coffee. Reece? Her heart did a loop-the-loop, and her resolve transported into the same expanse of time and space that her New Year's resolutions seemed to melt into every year between January tenth and the fifteenth. And in this case, her pride quickly followed.

A quick pat-down of her hair and a critical perusal in the hall mirror made her cringe. But Reece had seen her in the hospital, and she looked a lot better now than she had then. Of course, he hadn't been around since dropping her off, so maybe he couldn't take reality after all. Shaking her head, she pushed back the crazy thought. In her heart, she knew he was busy trying to crack this case before the culprit met his or her objective. But could she help it if she missed him?

She pasted on a smile, gathered a breath and opened the door. Then blinked in surprise. "Mr. Terrie?" The liaison from one of her possible church sponsors stood at her door, looking as though he had every right to be there. "Wh-what can I do for you?"

Mr. Terrie frowned. "I'm here to check your progress. Remember I called yesterday?"

"I'm sorry. I didn't receive the message." How could one of the girls take a message and not tell her about something this important? Her mind shot through the house, mentally assessing the neatness—or not—of each room.

Mr. Terrie remained on the porch, looking at her as though he wondered if she was going to let him in. Heat rushed to her cheeks, and she opened the door wider, stepping aside to allow entrance. "Please, come in."

For the next thirty minutes, Denni led him through the house, pinpointing areas where she, Reece and the girls had made improvements—from the repaired leaky faucets, to the new deck. She refrained from offering information about the fire and the gas leak. And he didn't ask.

At the end of the tour, Mr. Terrie pulled out a handkerchief and dabbed his forehead. He smiled at Denni and gave her a fatherly wink.

"I very much admire what you're trying to do here. It's not easy being a pioneer. I caught a glimpse of your revised proposal and I was impressed with your plans to integrate more ministry-minded programs such as pastoral counseling and group sessions with Christian-based counselors."

"Thank you, Mr. Terrie. To be honest, my vision wasn't quite that far-reaching until Elizabeth shared her concerns with me. And I have to admit I agreed with her. If the project is going to have the potential to change these girls' lives forever, I have to take more steps to provide for their spiritual growth. I'm glad you approve."

"I do. Very much and as far as I'm concerned, you have my recommendation for funding. I intend to make some calls and offer endorsement to the other churches considering your project and encourage them to do the same."

"Thank you, Mr. Terrie. I appreciate that more than you know."

Moments later, Denni showed him to the door, her heart lighter than it had been in days.

Mr. Terrie made good on his promise, and by the end of the day four more possible sponsors had called, congratulating her on receiving their support for the coming year.

"Cate," she said later as they prepared a light dinner for just the two of them. "What do you think about an open house?"

"What do you mean?"

"I think we should have an open house and invite the

sponsors and anyone else who might want to see what we're all about."

"Sounds all right. What have you heard from Miss Wilson?"

Denni heaved a sigh. She hadn't seen Elizabeth since the night of the birthday party. She knew Reece suspected the woman. "I don't know. The support we'll receive from the other churches will only equal what I get from our church. If we don't get the funding, we'll have to hold off on looking at property for at least another year."

"Denni?"

"Hmm?"

"Who do you think is behind all the stuff going on around here?"

Denni wanted to pretend the incidents were nothing more than accidents, but the time for burying her head in the sand was over. The attempt on her life was no accident.

"I just don't know."

The girl's eyes clouded with worry. "Do you think it's one of us?"

"Oh, Cate. I don't see how it could be." Denni smiled at her. "I know it wasn't you. I'm sure I could have taken you down pretty easily…considering your condition."

Cate laughed and flexed her muscles. "Not likely."

They both grew serious again. Cate set a bowl of salad on the table, then turned back to Denni. "It's weird to think that one of us might not be who we think."

"I know, Cate. But you shouldn't be worrying about things like that right now. Besides, there's no way to know if it was someone at the party. Remember the window was open in the basement. So someone might have come in that way. Reece has questioned everyone and apparently is satisfied."

Cate gave a snort. "Reece isn't going to be satisfied until someone is locked up for hurting you. He's just laying low, would be my guess."

Shuddering a breath, Denni nodded her agreement. "I know. Cate, who was home yesterday besides you?"

"In the daytime?"

"Yeah."

"Only Shelley and Leigh. Rissa had some books to return to the library, and Fran had that interview at Dr. Raymond's office. Why?"

She shrugged. "Just wondering. Mr. Terrie mentioned having spoken to me yesterday. So apparently he talked to one of them and assumed it was me. Whoever it was must have forgotten to mention it."

Cate studied her for a moment. It was clear that her mind was whirling…Leigh or Shelley? Had they done it deliberately or, as happened on occasion, merely forgotten to pass the word along?

They sat in silence over their meal, neither eating much.

Finally, Cate asked, "Do you mind if I beg off cleaning up? I don't feel real well."

Concern filled Denni. "Are you in labor?"

Cate shook her head. "No cramping or anything. I'm just so tired."

"It won't be long now."

A little sigh escaped Cate and sadness crossed her features. "I know."

"Are you sure you want to give up the baby, Cate? It's not set in stone, you know."

"I do know. And ever since I started praying again

and reading my Bible, I don't know…I can't explain it…I just know it's the right thing to do." Her eyes misted and she placed a protective hand on her belly. "But I will miss this little one every day of my life."

Affection for the girl rose up in Denni. She crossed the room and gathered Cate in her arms, holding her while the pregnant girl sobbed. When Cate's tears were spent, Denni held her at arm's length. "You go ahead upstairs and lie down. Yell if you need me."

Realizing her own body was beginning to lose steam, Denni washed up the few dishes from their meager fare and wandered upstairs. She changed into a pair of comfy sweats and a T-shirt, grabbed her Bible, and headed for bed.

She was just dozing off when the doorbell rang. With a start, she pushed off the comforter and padded out into the hall and down the stairs to the front door. One of the girls must have forgotten her key.

Pulling back the curtain covering the small triangle window, she gasped at the sight of Reece standing there. She flung open the door.

Without waiting for an invitation, he strode right in. He took her by the arms and his gaze bore down on her, as though trying to read into her soul.

"Reece," she choked out. "What's wrong?"

"I can't wait another second," he rasped. And as though his emotions were more than he could take, he pulled her into a fierce hug.

Fear and excitement fired up inside Denni and she clung to Reece, determined that she would stay pure no matter how much she cared for him.

"Reece," she whispered. "I—I can't…"

He pulled away and peered into her eyes, confusion

clouding his. Then he smiled. "You think I meant I wanted to take you upstairs?"

Heat seared Denni's cheeks. "I'm sorry. I just assumed. I'm stupid. Of course that wasn't it."

Reece pressed a kiss to her forehead. "I'm a man, Denni. And I love you. It's a given that I'd want more than kisses and hugs. But I'm not a Neanderthal. I can control myself." He gave her a lopsided grin.

Denni's stomach turned over and she wanted to sink to the floor. "Then, what?"

"Honey, I need you to help me find God."

Denni's breath caught in her throat as joy bubbled to the surface. "Oh, Reece. That, I can definitely do."

Reece felt the wonder of peace for the first time in his memory. It was as though every instant of his life had led him to this moment. He finally understood how empty he was. He'd shed real tears when he'd prayed with Denni. Even now, before his cheeks were completely dry, he didn't feel shame. Only peace and an inexplicable joy…optimism—and he'd never really been an optimistic kind of guy.

"You're smiling again." Denni's soft voice caught his attention.

He snatched up her hand and laced his fingers with hers. "I'll probably never frown again."

"That works for me."

Reece squeezed her hand as his gaze caressed her face. She hadn't asked questions, but had simply granted his request and walked him through a meeting with his Savior. But he wanted her to know what had brought him to this place.

"My foster brother died in prison a few days ago."

A tiny gasp escaped her lips and she covered their joined hands. "I'm so sorry. Were you close?"

Shaking his head, Reece said flatly. "He killed our foster parents. I've hated him ever since—until the day before yesterday." He told of his meeting with the chaplain of the prison. "He gave some of Jonathon's letters to me—that I had returned unopened. And his Bible. I wanted to leave them, but something inside me compelled me to open that Bible. Do you know what Jonathon's favorite verse was?"

Denni shook her head.

"The same one I read to Cate at the hospital."

"Oh, Reece."

"When I saw that, I realized that Jonathon had read the verse just like I had, and just like Cate had. It was hard to swallow at first. I was angry with God, because if I wasn't an accident, then neither was Jonathon. And if he wasn't, then God had purposely created the man who had killed the only parents who ever loved me. I felt betrayed. Just as betrayed by God as by Jonathon."

Denni tightened her grip on his hand, encouraging him to continue.

"Everyone said Jonathon was dangerous. A time bomb just ticking away. But we didn't believe it. I figured he was all mouth. And the Ides believed that giving him real love would calm him. Change him. But that didn't mean they would put up with just anything. A couple of nights before he killed them, they had found a joint in our room. Jonathon had just turned eighteen a few days earlier, so they told him he would have to move out. He was packing his bag…"

Swallowing hard, Reece fought against the image filling his mind. The wild eyes. *I'll kill them.*

He shook his head. "He told me what he was going to do. And I thought he was all talk. And then two nights later, he broke in looking for money. When Thomas woke up, Jonathon killed him. Lydia apparently woke up too. I heard her scream, but by the time I got there, she was dead. He stared at me. Reminded me that he'd said he was going to kill them. Then he left. I don't know why he didn't kill me too. I think the cops half believed we were in it together. But my story held."

Denni's warm cheek rested against his shoulder. "I'm so sorry you had to go through all of that. No wonder you have such a hard time believing my girls are innocent."

"The hardest thing for me all of these years has been the guilt of believing that I might have stopped the killings if I'd gone to the police when Jonathon first said he'd kill them."

"But you couldn't have known. And it's doubtful they'd have taken you seriously anyway." She nudged him. "You know how cops are."

Reece smiled, appreciating her attempt to lighten the mood. "I carried the guilt until today when I read a letter he had written to me." Pulling it out of his windbreaker pocket, Reece read aloud.

Somewhere in my heart, I know that you blame yourself for not telling the police about the night I left the house. But one absolutely had nothing to do with the other. I was only spouting off out of hurt when I said that to you. I had no intention of ever going back to the house. But I was coming down from a high and wanted another fix. I wasn't thinking straight and I was out of money. I knew where Lydia hid her Christmas money—

that's what I broke in for. Not to hurt them. But Thomas woke up and came after me. Like any man would to protect his family. I snapped. And you know the rest. It would be too much to ask that you forgive me. But I do hope you'll forgive yourself.

Reece drew a ragged breath.

Denni lifted her head from his shoulder and peered into his eyes. "Do you forgive yourself, Reece?"

"As much as I can, for now," he said honestly. "One step at a time."

"Denni?"

Reece glanced up at the sound of the frail voice to find Cate standing in the doorway.

Denni jumped to her feet. "Is it the baby?"

Cate nodded. "My water just broke."

Chapter Twenty-One

"What do you mean she doesn't work there?" Denni all but yelled into the receiver. "Leigh has been working at the Barbecue Shack for the past three years. Put her on the phone!" New waitresses. *What's the point of even letting them answer the phone? They never know anything.*

The pause that followed soothed Denni's ruffled feathers until a voice—not Leigh's—spoke.

"Denni, is that you?"

"Mike? Where's Leigh?"

"What do you mean?"

"Leigh!"

"I know who she is, but why would she be here?"

Oh, brother. Like she really had time for twenty questions when Cate was dilating at this very moment and needed Denni's hand to hold.

"She's working?" Duh!

"Look, Denni. I don't want to get involved in anything between the two of you, but Leigh quit here about three months ago. I told her she'd either have to quit the

Glass Slipper or here. I just didn't want men from that crowd recognizing her and causing a scene."

Denni gulped, her mind trying to wrap around two things…one, Leigh had been lying to her for months. Two. Oh, Leigh…the Glass Slipper? Tears stung Denni's eyes.

"But I call your restaurant every month to make sure everything is going fine. It's part of my agreement with the girls when they move into the house."

"I'll look into that. Leigh still has friends who work here—including some of the managers. One of them could be lying for her. I'm sorry."

"It's okay, Mike. Thanks." She replaced the black pay-phone receiver into the cradle and walked back toward the nurse's station to find out if Cate was settled in enough for her to go and sit with her. She turned as Reece came up behind her. "Okay, the truck is parked as close as I could get. How is she?"

"I don't know yet," Denni said, unable to muster much enthusiasm.

"Hey, don't worry. She's going to be fine." He slipped his arm around her.

"I know. It's not Cate."

Pressure on her shoulder halted her. She turned to face him.

"What is it?"

"Leigh."

"Is she okay?"

Denni shook her head, biting her lip to stop the trembling. "I called her at work to let her know about Cate."

Reece groaned and rubbed his hand over his shaven head.

A frown creased Denni's brow. "What?"

"I assume you mean that you called the barbecue place?"

"Yes. Where else? Did you know something about Leigh that I didn't know?"

"Most likely. I learned about her 'dancing career' the other night. Sean was called to the Glass Slipper to break up a fight, and Leigh was in the big middle of it."

Disbelief and a sense of betrayal threatened to overwhelm her already taut nerves. "And you didn't see fit to tell me?"

"She got fired on the spot. I assumed she'd tell you."

"So you protected her secret?" A short laugh spurted from Denni's lips. "Since when are you two so chummy?"

Reece's eyebrows narrowed. "Would you rather we were fighting?"

"You should have told me."

"I disagree. I gave her my word."

But you're supposed to love me.

"Are you two with Cate Sheridan?" A petite blond nurse looked between them, her expression clearly telling them to knock it off and go support the young woman in pain.

Denni nodded. "Is she ready for us to come sit with her?"

"Yes. She's not too far dilated. It'll be a few hours yet, most likely. First babies take their time."

The nurse waved them toward Cate's room and they proceeded down the hall in tense silence. Reece cleared his throat. "Have you gotten in touch with anyone else?"

Denni glared at him, wishing she had the right to give him the silent treatment, but knowing in her heart that he had done the right thing as far as Leigh was concerned. Also, she couldn't help but respect him for it.

"No. The girls still aren't home. I left a message on the machine. I hope someone will listen to it and let everyone else know."

"I'll keep trying," he assured her. "I'll be back later."

She opened the door to Cate's sweet pink-yellow-and-blue-decorated birthing room—her home away from home for the next twenty-four to forty-eight hours.

Denni didn't want to think about the emptiness Cate was going to feel when she left the hospital without her baby.

When she walked in the room, the girl was beaming—far from the pain-ravaged demeanor Denni had been expecting—but then, she'd never been around a woman in labor before.

An IV line hung from a steel post next to the bed, and Cate had changed into a pink hospital gown. She was sitting up, and the TV was on, but muted. She patted her protruding belly. "They said I can keep her in the room with me after she's born."

"Does the hospital know you're giving her up?"

Cate nodded. "The Michaelsons are still in Nicaragua on a missions trip. They won't be home for two days and they told Mrs. Johnson they don't mind if I spend time with the baby. As a matter of fact, they want to make sure I really want to give her up since they've been to this same place in the process three times and the birth mothers all decided to keep their babies."

"I'm happy for you, honey." Denni held her hand. "Are you sure it won't be harder for you to let her go if you spend that much time with her?"

"I'm sure. Giving her up is the right choice. It's not the easy choice. But it is the right one." Her face contorted with pain, and she began to blow.

Denni counted and waited until the contraction was over. "I'm proud of you, Cate. Really."

Tears pooled in Cate's eyes. "I made such a mess of things. But knowing that God created my baby and has a great life planned for her gives me hope."

For the next couple of hours, they talked and dreamed aloud, until the contractions grew closer together and more severe. The medicine the nurse shot into the IV to ease some of the pain began to take effect and Cate's eyes drooped, until finally her soft snoring signaled that she had fallen asleep.

Denni watched the sitcom playing out on the silent TV, and read the closed-captioned subtitles.

Movement at the long, thin window on the door caught her attention. The door opened, and the four girls peeped inside. Denni pressed her index finger to her lips and motioned them to stay in the hall.

"How's she doing?" Shelley asked.

"She's sleeping right now. The nurse said she's a little over halfway there. Everything seems to be right on target. Did you all get the news at the same time?"

Shelley shook her head. "Fran got the message you left on the machine at home, and she called Rissa at her singles' meeting at church. She called me at work, and I called Leigh at work."

Denni's gaze shifted to Leigh. "I tried to call your work too."

The girl's eyes grew wide and her cheeks bloomed with color. "Denni…"

"Why didn't you tell me you quit the Barbecue Shack?"

Shelley cleared her throat loudly and looked at the other two girls. "Cate's sleeping anyway, so how about we head to the cafeteria?"

"Good idea, sweetie," Rissa said, a little too brightly. "I'm famished."

Fran glanced from Leigh to Denni. "Don't say anything you'll regret, okay? Take it from someone who can't keep her foot out of her mouth. It's not worth it later."

Denni squeezed her hand. "Thanks, Fran. I'll keep that in mind."

After the trio headed down the hall, stopping at the nurse's station for directions, Denni turned to Leigh. "Let's go to the waiting area so we can sit down to discuss this."

The mauve vinyl chairs seemed even colder than usual as Denni sat on a loveseat and patted the cushion next to her.

"Before you say anything, I just want you to know that I haven't danced anywhere else since I got fired. I've been hostessing at the country club."

A breath whispered through Denni's lips. Relief that she wouldn't have to issue an ultimatum. Still, she had questions. "Why would you quit the Barbecue Shack and go to work for someplace so…dark?"

"I have bills to pay and this was the quickest way to make the most money and still convince myself I could hold onto my dignity. I figured at least I wasn't hooking." She leaned forward, resting her elbows on her knees and to Denni, she looked so very young. "I was kidding myself. Every night for the past six months I've felt as though a weight hung around my neck. Not only for lying to you, but just the whole atmosphere in there made me feel gross."

"Why did you need extra money, Leigh?"

A look of dread sifted over Leigh's features. "I don't want to tell you this…"

They were both crying by the time Leigh finished telling Denni why. "Oh, Leigh. You've had to bear the miscarriage all alone. That's why you were using drugs last year? If only I'd known." If only she'd had the kind of counseling she was about to implement for the girls.

Leigh's face bore a look of utter surprise. "You feel sorry for me?"

Denni braced for a confrontation. "Not sorry, exactly. I just wish I could have been there for you. If I'd known the heartache you were living all this time, I would have been." She drew a sharp breath at the tears streaming down Leigh's cheeks. "Honey, don't you know how much I love you?"

Leigh leaned over and wrapped her arms around Denni, as a child would her mother. She rested her head on Denni's shoulder and sobs racked her body. "I thought you'd hate me for getting pregnant."

"I could never hate you. Do I hate our little Catie?"

"There have been so many times I wanted to come to you and talk. But I didn't want to have to tell you about losing my scholarship."

Denni squeezed her. "All right. We'll move on from here, okay? But we have to talk about reestablishing trust between us. Can we do that?"

Leigh nodded. "So Corrigan didn't tell you, huh?"

Denni shook her head. "I found out tonight when I called Mike at the Shack. That's when Reece admitted to knowing." She smiled. "And he didn't apologize for not telling me, either."

Leigh chuckled, swiping at the tears on her cheeks. "He didn't want to promise. I could tell he felt like he was betraying you. The guy's not so bad."

"Seriously? Because I plan to keep him around."

"So, it's L-O-V-E is it?"

Heat washed Denni's cheeks. "Maybe."

A shrug lifted Leigh's slender shoulders. "I guess he's okay. But you know he doesn't go to church. I thought that was a no-no."

So she had been listening…

Denni grinned, and joy bubbled inside her at the memory of Reece's newfound commitment to Christ. "Well, guess what? That's about to change."

A questioning frown creased Leigh's brow. "You know something I don't know. I can tell."

"I guess he wouldn't mind if I told you. Reece became a Christian tonight."

Leigh's jaw dropped open. "No!"

"Yes, ma'am," a male voice behind them startled both women. "I am a bona fide Bible-thumper now."

Leigh rolled her eyes. "As if you weren't bad enough, before."

"You're back. Did you check on Cate?"

"The nurse said they're going to examine her."

"I can't believe she's finally having the baby."

Reece chuckled and nudged Leigh's shoulder. "You survived the Denni-nator, I see. You almost got me in big trouble with that whole secret."

Denni stood and stretched. "She's fine. And so are you. Leigh told me everything."

Approval shone in Reece's eyes. "Where's Sean tonight?"

Leigh's cheeks turned red. "I haven't seen him much since Denni's party. He's pretty mad at me."

"Give him a chance. I think he's kind of crazy about you."

"We'll see if he hangs around once he finds out for sure I'm not the guilty party in all the House stuff."

Reece's brow rose. "You figured that out, huh?"

"Do I look stupid?" Leigh said, a snort leaving her pierced nose. "Believe me. I knew what Sean was up to the first time he asked me out." She grinned. "Of course, he couldn't resist me, so it became real whether he likes it or not. But we have a lot to talk about."

"I just wanted to let you know, it's time." The little blond nurse who had been with them since they'd checked Cate in nodded to Denni and handed her a medical cap and gown. "Cate wants you in there with her. You'll need to put these on."

Denni felt the excitement and sadness associated with the end of one thing and the beginning of something else. For Cate. The end of this pregnancy meant the first day of the rest of her life. For the baby it meant going to parents who had waited for her for who knew how long?

For Denni. Well, tonight, everything had changed. The possibilities were endless.

She slipped on the gown and turned to Reece. He stared back with such tenderness it took her breath from her lungs.

He winked and gave her an encouraging nod.

All they needed now was to find out who wanted her dead.

Chapter Twenty-Two

Denni opened her eyes, not sure what had awakened her. Sunlight danced on her bedroom ceiling, and she smiled at the various shapes reflected by the items in her room.

Lazily, she stretched beneath the cozy covers and remembered why she was lying in bed when the sun was out with such force. Cate's baby girl had been born at 4:13 a.m. Weighing in at seven pounds, two ounces, she was a darling baby. One of the prettiest Denni had ever seen.

The memory of Cate snuggling her daughter brought a tear to Denni's eye. She had watched the new mother closely, looking for signs that she wouldn't be able to give the infant up when the time came. But so far, there didn't seem to be any weakening of her resolve. Only sadness and a lot of awe that she had given birth to the tiny life.

The downstairs phone rang, and the padding of feet on the carpeted steps followed. A moment later, Denni heard a light tap. The hinges creaked as someone opened the door.

"I'm awake," Denni said. "You can come in."

Rissa's grinning face peeked in. "Hey, glad I didn't wake you."

"Nope. I've been lying here watching the sun-shapes on my ceiling. Who was on the phone?"

"Oh, yeah." Rissa rolled her eyes. "I nearly forgot. That was Cate."

Denni frowned, pushing back the covers as she sat up. "Is everything okay?"

"Oh, the baby's fine and so is Cate. She just wants that baby blanket she got from her mama when she was little. She said she washed it and tucked it on the top shelf of her closet."

Alarm seized Denni. "What does she want with the blanket? Did she say?"

Rissa shrugged her plump shoulders. "I think she wants to give it to the adoptive parents—so that the little darling knows her real mama loved her." She frowned and peered closer at Denni. "You don't think she wants to keep the baby for herself do you?"

"I don't know. It's possible, I suppose."

"Anyway, I'm running so-o-o late for work. Can you please get the blanket out of the closet and take it when you go see Cate later?"

"Of course." Denni was already headed for the chest of drawers to grab her clothes for the day. "Can I take my time, drink a cup of coffee, maybe fix a little breakfast, or is Cate alone and needing company?"

Rissa waved her hands. "Oh, Cate said Shelley was down at the cafeteria getting some food, and when she gets back, she'll look after the baby so Cate can take a shower."

"Okay good. I need a nice long shower, myself." She

grinned at Rissa, who, despite being "late for work" was still standing in the doorway chatting.

Rissa sniffed and started to turn away. Then she swung back around with a teasing grin. "You two seemed pretty chummy last night. Anything I should know about?"

"I thought you were late. When I have news I feel you should be in on, I promise, I'll tell you."

Drawing herself up in mock offense, Rissa spun on her heel. "All right, fine. I can take a hint," she tossed over her shoulder.

Denni shook her head, smiling at the girl's antics. Gathering up her clothes, she headed to the bathroom. She felt infinitely better after the steaming water loosened up her stiff muscles.

When she reached the bedroom Cate shared with Shelley, she remembered the baby blanket. She opened the door, scowling at the clutter. Stepping over a stack of magazines, she made a mental note to have another talk with Shelley about picking up after herself. The girl had a lot of great qualities…neatness wasn't one of them. Poor Cate. Neatness just happened to be one of the great qualities she did possess. Shelley's tendency to laziness drove her crazy.

Denni's lip twitched as she crossed to the closet. "Oh, brother, more clutter." Looking up to the shelf, she spied the baby blanket at the bottom of a stack of shoeboxes, winter sweaters, and several college textbooks that Shelley, the packrat, felt she couldn't live without after the semester.

Gathering a deep breath, Denni reached up and snagged the blanket, pushing on the stack of items with the other hand. The pile shifted balance with Denni's next tug on the blanket. She screeched and covered her head with her arms as the entire contents of the shelf tumbled down. When the onslaught ended, she was none the worse for wear, but she was highly irritated that the shelf had been so poorly organized as to have toppled in the first place.

With jerky movements and a ticked-off huff, she bent over and started the chore of cleaning up her mess—although she felt, in this instance, she would be well within her rights to forego that particular house rule.

She was just about to give in to the impulse and let the girls reorganize properly, when her gaze fell on a familiar document. A shoebox, tilted on its side, had spilled its entire contents onto the gray carpet. Denni's lips trembled as she bent down and retrieved the application for the grant. Every page was scribbled on with a variety of colors. She glanced closer and deciphered the scrawls on the page. It wasn't mere scribbling. But one word repeated over and over. NO! NO! NO!

Why would Shelley or Cate want to keep her from getting the funding to keep the house open and buy a couple more? They had nothing to gain, but they had their home to lose by sabotaging her efforts.

A gasp flew from her lips. The room began to spin crazily. The image of fires and a flooded basement invaded her mind. She sank to her knees, her palm pressed to her racing heart.

Sabotage? *Oh, Lord. Please no. Not one of my girls.*

Cate or Shelley. Tears of horror raced down her cheeks. One of her girls wanted her dead.

Reece!

Grabbing the application, Denni flew down the

stairs to the kitchen. She snatched up the receiver and called the police station. A squeaky-voiced officer answered.

"I need to speak to Reece!" she commanded, hearing the hysteria in her voice.

"Who, ma'am?"

"Detective Reece Corrigan. Get him! This is Denni Mahoney and he will want to speak with me."

The dispatcher stepped away from the phone. Three minutes later, he returned. "I'm sorry, ma'am, the detective is out. Give me your name and number and I'll give him the message as soon as he's back at the station."

"Does he have his cell phone?"

"Sorry, ma'am. I can't give out that information."

"Never mind," she snapped. "I'll find him myself."

Reece drew a sharp breath and asked her one more time. "Why doesn't anyone remember seeing you out back at the fence?"

Elizabeth glared. "Because, Detective, I left when everyone was headed outside to admire your handiwork."

"Without saying goodbye to the birthday girl?"

"As a matter of fact I did say goodnight to her. She had just told her father's fiancée that they were out of soda."

Truth registered through Reece. "You didn't mention that before."

"I just remembered." Elizabeth moved away from her desk and lowered herself into a chair next to Reece. "Listen, Detective. I am fully aware that you know about my months in rehab. It's true that Denni was the one who was forced to turn me down for a child. But I know she was only doing her job. I am not suffering from some kind of vendetta against her. Denni walked me to the door the night of her party. She closed the door behind me. I am not guilty."

Reece stood. If his instincts panned out, then this woman was innocent. And that led his investigation straight back to the girls.

She made herself small against the side of the building as Denni's car pulled into the parking garage. The baby nuzzled against her, smelling fresh and sweet. Oh, Mother would be so completely happy. They would be a family. And Denni Mahoney would never take this little girl from her mommy.

"No, she won't, my sweet little girl," she said to the baby.

Denni's car disappeared around the concrete wall and she took her opportunity. Clutching the baby tightly against her breast, she slid into the caged elevator and took it to the next level. She breathed a sigh of relief as the doors opened and there was no sign of Denni or anyone else. She hurried to her car and slipped inside, glad now that she'd forgotten to lock the doors. Carefully, she laid her new baby sister in the seat next to her. Oh but, a baby should be restrained in a car seat.

Well, she'd be careful. She'd never been in an accident before, so odds were she wouldn't be now. She fired up the engine, and, within seconds, drove into the bright day.

Mother would be so proud of her.

"Denni! She's gone!" Cate's pink robe hung open over her hospital gown and her bare feet padded against the tile as she raced down the hall when Denni stepped off the elevator.

"Who is? Cate, what's wrong?"

"My baby. She's gone. I left her with Shelley and went to take a shower, but when I got back, they were both gone."

A sense of dread gnawed low in Denni's stomach and began to rise. "Wait. Maybe the staff took her to weigh her or something. And Shelley went to get a snack out of the machine or—or coffee."

"No! And don't you dare defend her this time. My baby is weighed in my room every few hours. She's never supposed to leave me."

"All right, honey. Calm down. Have you reported her absence to the nurses?"

"She just did." A tall, slender African-American nurse slammed down the phone and stood to her full height behind the nurse's station. "Security has been alerted and the hospital is being locked down as we speak. No one will be allowed in or out."

Cate's face twisted and sobs racked her body. "Denni...I think Shelley stole my baby! Do you...think she's stopped taking her medicine again?"

Denni placed an arm about the distraught young woman's shoulders and led her back to her room. She tried to wrap her mind around the slightest possibility that Shelley could be guilty of such a thing.

"Cate, we know Shelley." Denni's voice sounded flat, but she felt compelled at least to try to defend the girl who had been one of those closest to her. She'd known Shelley since the girl had first entered the foster-care system over ten years ago. "She's never pretended to want a baby." Just the opposite, in fact.

"I know, but she just kept babbling on about how pretty the baby is and how much her mother would love to see her. Do you think…maybe she stopped taking her medicine again?"

"Her mother?" Alarm shot through Denni. Panic began to rise. "She takes her medicine every day. I watch her do it after the last time she stopped taking it."

"Then why else would she do this?"

"I don't know, Cate, honey. But I'm going to find out. I need to go."

"What do you mean? You can't leave me alone." Cate's tears started afresh. "Besides, they won't let you out. Denni, what do you think is going on? I can tell there's something. You do think Shelley is hallucinating again!"

"Pray, Cate. Just pray."

Denni grabbed her purse and ran for the door.

At the elevator, she pressed the button. She paced in front of the double doors and stopped, bouncing on her toes. The longer she had to wait for the stupid elevator, the longer a mentally unstable young woman had possession of a defenseless baby. In a normal state, Shelley wouldn't hurt a fly, but in her present state, if she hadn't been taking her meds, anything was surely possible. It just depended on what sort of mood her "mother" was in. Shelley had done crazy things, mostly self-destructive, such as jump out of a tree and break her arm, while listening to someone she thought was her mother.

Oh, Father. Protect Cate's baby.

She pressed the elevator button again and again.

"There's no sense in pushing buttons."

Denni glanced around to face the stern African-American nurse. "Power has been cut to the elevators."

"Fine, I'll take the stairs."

She had to stop at the entrance to the stairway and show her ID. Still the tall, twenty-something security guard didn't want to let her go.

"Nurse," she called down the hall.

"I told you."

"Well, tell *him* that I am a friend of the kidnapped baby's mother, please."

The nurse heaved a sigh and nodded. "She couldn't have done it."

He shrugged. "They're not going to let you out of the building anyway. So you're just wasting your time."

Denni twisted her lips into a scowl. "Thanks for the tip, Barney Fife."

Anger shot to his eyes, and Denni hurried through the door before he could stop her on principle.

She encountered the same problem at the ground floor. "Look, I'm not the kidnapper. I'm the baby's mother's friend. Call up to the fourth floor and ask for the nurse taking care of the baby's mother."

He did so.

"Too bad you guys weren't so gung ho about doing your job an hour ago!"

Reece heard the call over the radio and knew…

A baby stolen from the hospital. Possible suspect, a teenage girl who fitted Shelley's description to a T.

He grabbed his cell phone just as it rang. "Denni? I just heard the call come in. It was Shelley?"

"Yes, Reece. Listen. You have to come to the hospital and get me out of here. It's locked down. They're not going to let me out. Even the elevators have been disabled. I had to take the stairs down from the fourth floor, and I'm at the emergency entrance. Make sure you have your badge so you can show the security guard."

"All right. I'm on my way."

Twenty minutes later, Denni slid into the passenger seat of Reece's car. "Head toward Fourth and Grand, there's an old abandoned apartment building there. I think that's where Shelley took the baby."

"What for?"

"Shelley's talking to her mother again."

"That's not a good thing?"

"Her mother's dead. She OD'd on heroine when Shelley was four. Shelley was alone in the house with her mother's body until she got so desperate to eat that she had to venture out. A neighbor found her digging in a Dumpster and called the police."

Reece grimaced at the image of the little girl, alone in an apartment with a corpse for a week. His mind swirled with questions as he turned the unmarked car toward Fourth and Grand.

"She seemed to adjust all right until she was around ten. The family she'd been staying with for six years was transferred to Denver and she was sent to another foster home. The loss of her family sent her over the edge."

"They couldn't adopt her?"

Denni hesitated. "Let's just say they chose not to."

"What do you mean by 'over the edge'?"

"She started seeing and talking to her mother. One night, she attempted suicide, but her foster parents found her in time. There was an empty pill bottle on the bed next to her, and a suicide note that said her mother had told her to do it. Fortunately, they got her to the hospital in time. She's been taking medicine for years to suppress psychotic hallucinations. I watch her take them daily, but she must have been just pretending. I don't know why.

"There's Shelley's car. Hurry up and pull over, Reece."

"Wait for me, Denni."

But he spoke into an empty seat as Denni sprang from the car and ran toward the entrance of the abandoned building. Muttering an oath, then a quick repentance as he remembered his new faith and his conscience pricked him, he slammed the car into Park and followed.

Chapter Twenty-Three

Denni gathered a slow breath and prayed harder than she'd ever prayed in her life. The now-abandoned building had no outside door, so she went in through the gaping space, trying to remember the layout as it had been when Shelley was little. She'd been the social worker on the scene, new to her job and ready to make a difference in the lives of abused and neglected children. Shelley's soulful eyes and the signs of more maturity than a little girl should have to possess had drawn Denni from day one. She'd watched over her as much as possible and probably beyond what any other social worker would have done.

Led by memories that spanned fifteen years, Denni headed for the stairs at the end of the hall and ascended toward the apartment where Shelley had spent those few terrifying days and nights alone with her mother's lifeless body.

Oh, Lord why didn't I know she was only pretending to take that medicine? Had she been so wrapped up in the need for finances and wanting to build that she'd neglected the needy ones right in front of her eyes? She continued to climb, and her thoughts went to Leigh. Once again, she felt a prick of remorse. How could she have been so consumed by her own needs that she'd lost sight of her real purpose in the first place? What good would she have done if she'd built a dozen houses, but lost the first precious girls God had entrusted to her care?

She heard talking as she approached the second-floor hallway. Did Shelley have an accomplice?

"Mommy, why are you so mad at me? I did as you asked. Why won't you even look at the baby?"

A silent pause.

"But she's beautiful too. Much prettier than I ever was. M-maybe you'll love her better. You could hold her and tell her stories and brush her hair."

Another pause.

Denni heard boots scrape against the concrete steps. She turned to find Reece scowling at her. She put her finger to her lips. She glanced inside and relief flowed through her that Shelley hadn't noticed the noise.

They listened to the one-sided conversation. Mewling noises came from the baby.

"Mommy," Shelley said, her voice trembling. "I—I can't do that. It would hurt her."

Denni's eyes widened as she turned to Reece. He scowled and motioned her to get out of the way. His hand was ready on his gun. Denni grabbed his wrist. "Don't hurt her," she whispered.

"I'll do my best."

"Of course I love you, Mommy, and I know you love me, but why do you want me to throw the baby away? Can't I just take her back to Cate?"

Tears pooled in Denni's eyes at the state the girl was in.

"Shelley," Reece's voice was calm. "It's Detective Corrigan. I'm coming in."

"N-no. M-mommy says you mustn't bother me." Her eyes were wide with fear. Denni stepped into the room after Reece. Shelley's face contorted in rage. "You have to leave. You can't take the baby away from our mommy."

"Shelley, honey. The baby belongs to Cate, remember? She misses her terribly."

"Liar! Cate doesn't want her. She's giving her away. My mommy would never give away her baby."

"Your mommy is dead, Shelley. Remember?"

Confusion flashed across Shelley's face. She cocked her head as though listening.

"Why, Denni? Why do you want to take me away from Mommy again?"

The words hit Denni like a blow to the gut. "Shelley," she breathed. "Honey, I didn't take you from your mommy. Your mother died from an overdose. Remember? Think. That woman talking to you isn't your mom. She's only in your head."

Shelley, babe in her arms, began to back away toward the glassless window. She glanced out to the street. Her eyes were filled with tears when she looked back at the empty space she'd been talking to. "I don't want to, Mommy."

Denni saw what Shelley intended to do. Panic seized her. *Oh, God, protect that baby, please.*

Throughout the conversation, Reece had slowly inched his way toward Shelley, but he was still too far away to do any good. A muscle twitched in his jaw as he focused on the job ahead.

Denni took a step closer to keep Shelley's attention diverted. "Shelley, honey. Please don't hurt the baby."

"You don't care! You don't care!"

"Of course I do. I never want to see a child harmed. If you throw the baby down, she's going to die. Do you understand that?"

Shelley jerked her head toward the empty space, confusion clouding her eyes.

Reece took the moment to inch closer to the girl. He motioned to Denni to keep talking.

"Your mother was a good woman," Denni said. "Would she ask you to hurt yourself or the baby? Think, Shelley. That's not your mother talking to you. She loved you."

Shelley paused.

"No," she said to the air. "Y-you're not my mother." She paused again. Then looked back at Denni. Her brow furrowed as she seemed to be looking between two women, trying to decide who was lying.

"Mommy? D-don't leave me again. No, I don't love her more. I'll do it. See?"

She rushed toward the window, just as Reece wrapped his arms around her and the baby, pulling her back.

Shelley screamed, kicking at Reece. "Mommy, don't go! Don't leave me again! I tried to be a good girl. I tried." Sobs racked her as she wilted in Reece's arms.

Denni stepped forward and took the wailing baby. "Shhh, sweetie. It's okay. We'll get you back where you belong soon." She nuzzled the baby until she quieted.

Reece kept his arms around Shelley. The girl didn't struggle as he led her to his car. Denni could see he didn't want to handcuff her, but he had no choice. He called the station and let them know the baby had been found and that he needed an ambulance for the kidnapper.

Less than thirty minutes later, Denni placed the baby in Cate's arms.

One week later

Denni had felt Reece's tension during their earlier phone conversation. She'd been dreading their expected date this evening, anticipating the it's-not-you-it's-me brush-off. Still, she couldn't stop her heart from racing when his truck pulled into the drive. She opened the door before he made it to the porch. Better just to confront the issue and get it over with.

In the early-summer evening, just a hint of rain plumped the clouds, mingling its fragrance with the roses planted at the bottom of the steps on either side of the walkway.

She stopped short when she saw the bouquet of wildflowers he carried.

"Are those for me?"

A knee-weakening smile lifted the corners of his mouth. "Who else?"

Denni's neck muscles relaxed, and she stepped aside to allow him into the house. Her pulse quickened as he bent down and pressed a quick kiss to her lips.

"Flowers, Corrigan?" Leigh's voice acted like a water hose, dousing the moment before the kiss could get any better. "Who are you trying to impress?"

"I thought you had a date with Sean," Reece said, a scowl marring his handsome features.

"I do. Later." She flopped down on the sofa and picked up the TV remote.

With a frustrated growl, Reece grabbed Denni's hand. "Come with me." He pulled her outside to the front porch and stopped in front of the swing.

Bewildered, Denni sat on the swing and looked up at him expectantly. "What's wrong with you?"

He gathered a long, slow breath and shoved his hand into his pocket. Denni's eyes widened and the world took on a new look when he pulled out a black velvet box.

His eyes never faltered from hers, but his expression softened as he dropped down on one knee.

"Reece."

"I've never done this before, Denni. And I'm not a very sensitive guy. You know that. So if I do it all wrong, it'll serve me right if you say no."

Denni couldn't stop her itching fingers from reaching out and lightly touching his face. Emotion flickered in his eyes and he covered her hand with his, bringing it to his lips as he pressed a warm kiss to her palm.

"Will you marry me?"

A wave of joy swept over Denni. She laughed and cupped his face with her hands. "You know I will." Leaning forward she pressed her lips to his. He gathered her close and deepened their kiss, sealing their promise of forever.

When he pulled away and slipped the ring on her finger, the clouds released gentle drops.

And as Reece's mouth took hers in another warm tender kiss, Denni knew she would always love a summer rain.

Epilogue

Shelley Bartlett
C/o Lakewood Mental Facility
Lakewood, Mo.

September 10,

Dearest Shelley,
I was so thrilled to receive your last letter and to
hear how well things are going for you. I ache to
see you, and I'm waiting with anticipation for
your doctor to give the word that it would be in
your best interest for me to come visit.

To answer your big question: Of course I forgive you, honey. Don't you know how much I
love you?

You asked me to stop holding back in my letters to spare your feelings, so I'm going to tell you
everything from now on. Here's some good news!
Sean and Leigh eloped last night. Or is that bad
news? (Laughing here). Not a huge surprise at

any rate. They're crazy together. The odd couple to the extreme. But they love each other, and I guess that's the important thing. They went to meet Sean's parents and guess what? The couple adores our Leigh. But then, who wouldn't?

Fran is still working for the doctor, filing papers and answering phones. She's loving it, and they seem to like her work. Since she decided Jesus is real after all, her entire attitude has changed—well, she still has a temper, but she works hard to control it and it's clear that God is softening her. But you won't believe what she's decided she wants to do. Instead of medicine, she's decided to enter the police academy and become a cop. Reece couldn't be more proud. All the two of them talk about is the law.

You wouldn't recognize Rissa (until she starts talking with that accent of hers). She has lost fifteen pounds since she started dating the new youth minister at church. They're already talking about a Christmas engagement. That's a little soon if you ask me. I plan to wait until at least New Year's. (Laughing again).

Please stop worrying yourself about the baby. She's thriving in her new home. Her parents have been wonderful with Cate and they send pictures almost every week. They've named the baby Hannah Rose. Isn't that beautiful?

As for Cate, you have nothing to fear from her either. So please be at peace on that account. She prays for you every day, and told me recently that she can't wait for you to get well, so that you can come home. So you see, we're all ready for you to come back to us. Our family is incomplete without you here.

And yes, dearest Shelley. You are most welcome back home. Reece and I are waiting to set a date for the wedding, hoping you can be one of my bridesmaids. Know what's funny? Reece doesn't think he has enough male friends to escort all of you girls (and my two sisters) down the aisle, so we're thinking about splitting you up between us. Part of you will be "groomswomen." Who knows, maybe Reece will get a couple of more friends before we have to order the tuxes. But at least it's an option.

I need to close this letter. Elizabeth and I are going to lunch together today. Can you believe that? It was by her invitation this time, too. Oh, did I tell you? They've decided to approve funding after all. Apparently, the budget is so well-managed under Elizabeth that they can expand the benevolence program. I won't receive quite as much as last year, but with the other sponsors and the tons of donations that have come in since my sister Raven's news story about the house, we are well on our way to staffing the place.

Please pray that God will send the girls He has chosen to live at Mahoney House.

As for you, take one minute at a time. And come home to us when the time is right.

Denni

Denni folded the letter, licked the envelope and set it in her outgoing mail slot. She leaned back in her chair and looked out at the yard next door. Buffy yelped as she tried and failed to jump the fence.

A smile curved Denni's lips as Reece walked up to the fence to speak to Mrs. James.

Denni's heart swelled with love. She watched him politely smile and defer to the elderly woman. God had certainly brought him a long way in a very short time.

He turned, as if sensing her attention. When his eyes found hers, the love reflected there increased her pulse. He spoke something to Mrs. James and turned, heading toward the back door. Denni rose and met him halfway. They met in the kitchen. "Hi," Denni said, her breath caught in her throat.

Reece's arms encircled her, drawing her close. "I missed you."

"Me too," she murmured as he dipped his head and claimed her lips.

* * * * *

And now, turn the page for a sneak preview of
BETRAYAL OF TRUST, the final book in
THE MAHONEY SISTERS *miniseries by*
Tracey V. Bateman, part of Steeple Hill's exciting
new line, Love Inspired Suspense!

On sale in October 2005 from Steeple Hill Books.

Raven Mahoney's jaw dropped as the sickening thud of truth slammed her with the force of a Major League line drive to the gut. While she'd been playing the dutiful maid of honor and helping with wedding preliminaries for her sister, Denni, she'd just missed out on reporting the press conference of the year. As far as Raven was concerned, that smacked of injustice.

From the TV screen in Denni's living room, cameras flashed at dizzying intervals. Raven could almost feel the claustrophobia she experienced every time she stood among the crowd of reporters, fighting for the chance to ask a question.

And she almost always got her chance to ask the tough ones. But not so tough the speaker wouldn't respond. She knew her success was a nice combination of her looks (especially if the speaker were a guy) and her instincts about how to ask the right questions so they sounded less intimidating to the speaker. At thirty-five, she'd gained a lot of savvy in her field and she was ready to move one step up the ladder of success.

Only, the teenybopper on the screen in front of her was getting the story she, Raven, should be getting. Something akin to a growl rose in Raven's throat, and her predatory nature kicked in. *Enjoy the cameras while you can, little girl, because as soon as I get home, you are going down.*

Raven closed her eyes and imagined herself at that press conference. Where she wanted to be. Despite the jumble of cameras and elbows jamming into her head, she itched to be there in the thick of things. To prove, once again, her value to the station. Ten years on the job had to count for something, didn't it?

Her chest tightened and pressure began to build. But this time, the claustrophobia struck in the living room of her soon-to-be-wed sister's Victorian home. Being in the bosom of her loving family suddenly felt more like standing in a trash compactor as the walls inched closer and closer together until finally they squished her in the process. A familiar sentiment over the past few years. Since her mother's death, when she'd learned the truth about who Raven Mahoney really was.

In retrospect it had all made sense. But the revelation had only served to make her feel more like an outsider in the midst of this family—and all these years later, Mac still hadn't set the record straight. Nor had Raven. Mac had no idea she knew. And as angry as she was with him for keeping the truth from her, she didn't have the heart to confront him.

"I can't believe Matthew Strong is pulling out of the race." Keri, Raven's younger sister, married barely a year herself to her childhood sweetheart, flopped onto the overstuffed green couch next to Raven. "I was going to vote for that guy."

"Shhh!" Raven glared at her sister and pressed the volume-up button on the remote.

"Sheesh, so-rry."

"What's going on?" Middle sister Denni entered the room, her eyes on the TV.

"Shh, or you'll get your head yanked off," Keri said in an exaggerated whisper.

"I'll talk if I want. It's my house. Besides, I'm the bride and everyone must cater to my whims. So there." Denni stuck her tongue out at Raven.

Raven rolled her eyes at the childish gesture, but couldn't resist a smile before shifting her focus back to the TV.

Her claws extended at the sight of the so-called reporter staring out from the screen. Kellie Cruise, an upstart and a spoiled rotten brat—way too under-qualified and inexperienced to be covering a press conference. Especially one of this magnitude. But nepotism at its finest continued to be at work for the daughter of the news director. And Raven knew if she didn't act fast, the just-out-of-college kid was going to get Bruce King's job when he retired. The job that Raven wanted. Deserved.

"What's going on?" Mac Mahoney's booming hint of an Irish brogue filled the room.

"Shhh!" The three girls spoke in unison.

"Hey, now. Is that any way to speak to your father?" He scowled, but quieted as his attention turned to the blond, blue-eyed reporter wrapping up the breaking news coverage.

"We've been told that Mr. Strong will not be answering any questions on the subject of his withdrawal. Now or ever. His decision is final and is based on personal reasons which he apparently has no intention of revealing."

The camera shifted back to the studio where the white-haired, almost retired anchor stared out at the TV audience.

"There you have it, folks. In the political upset of the year, a candidate whom analysts and polls favored by a three-to-one margin has withdrawn his name from the race for senate with only six weeks left until the primary." The older gentleman heaved a sigh. "To reiterate… With no warning for his supporters and no explanation, Matthew Strong has pulled out of the race for the Missouri senate."

If he'd said "And may God help us all," Bruce couldn't have been more obviously biased. It was too apparent that he had had high hopes for Matthew's election to the senate. No matter how much she might agree, Raven couldn't help but be a bit irritated with his transparency. Part of good reporting was remaining detached, keeping your opinion carefully masked behind the facts and nothing else. Perhaps it was simply that after so many years behind that desk, Bruce didn't feel he had anything to hide—namely his opinion.

With a sigh, Raven switched off the set as regular programming resumed. Tense silence reigned in the room and she knew her family was struggling not to ask *the* question. Finally, she could take the tension no more and she shot to her feet. "Okay, yes. It's Matthew."

"Your Matthew?" Mac looked at her over half glasses.

"Yes." She rubbed her throbbing temple with the balls of her fingers in an attempt to ease the pressure. My Matthew. Regret for what might have been all those years ago shot through her. She hadn't allowed herself second guesses. No regretting her decision.